CLOUDS OVER FEATHERWOOD FALLS

FEATHERWOOD FALLS SERIES
BOOK 4

HEATHER REYBURN

Cover design: Patti Roberts (Paradox Book Cover Designs)

ISBN 978-0-6457440-0-2 Print Edition

Heather Reyburn

www.heatherreyburn.com

For Hilary
Thank you for your unwavering encouragement and
support

1

*S*cowling, Zoe kicked the empty soft-drink can. It bounced and clattered on the footpath, startling a scavenging pigeon. The bird launched itself upward to rest on the rusted gutter of an abandoned shop. In the building's vacant window, Zoe glimpsed herself—a thin, forlorn teenager in a shabby, navy-blue uniform.

The knot in Zoe's stomach tightened. For years, dawdling home from school and chatting with her best friends, Amy and Natalia, had been the highlight of her day. Their conversations had morphed from games and what they did on the weekend, to gossip about teachers, fashion, music, and boys as they'd grown up. Talking was good. By the time she and Amy said goodbye to Natalia, then parted company two blocks later, problems had been sorted and secrets shared.

Zoe would increase her pace and look forward to being greeted by the fragrant hints of what dinner might contain—and her mother's company.

Those days were gone. This year, she'd focused on her studies, choir practise on Tuesdays, tennis on Wednesdays, and an after-school maths class on Thursdays. Anything to delay the return home.

It was Friday, and with a boring weekend ahead of her, Zoe's mind wandered to the world she had created where she worked in a hospital and helped countless patients. They thanked her for her aid, gave her flowers, and spread the word about her amazing healing skills.

Her thoughts of an anticipated and successful career faded to the memory of her sixteenth birthday the previous week. Forgotten by her mother—the one person she'd believed would never forget such an important occasion—Zoe dwelt on the nicely wrapped book and box of chocolates Mrs Worth from across the hall had gently placed in her hands as she had fumbled for her door key. Not to mention the sparkly top her friends had given her before hustling her onto a bus and off to a surprise outing at a pretty café overlooking Brisbane River. The cosy celebration had included a milkshake and luscious chocolate cake—complete with sixteen sparkling candles–and floods of grateful tears.

Zoe approached the shabby building concealing

her and her mother's apartment. Set at the perimeter of inner-city Brisbane, where a conglomeration of high-rise apartments was rapidly overtaking the historic pre-war cottages, the converted factory had loomed, ugly. But for Zoe, it was home—for now.

ZOE CLIMBED THE STAIRS, her pulse racing. Perhaps today would be different. Perhaps a lasagne would be baking in the oven, or a cooked chicken and salad would be waiting for her in the fridge?

Hope rose as she slid her key into the lock. Music drifted through the door and ... could that be her mother singing?

It is!

Catherine Ferguson sprang toward her daughter, arms outstretched.

Blinking rapidly, Zoe sank into her mother's embrace, leaned on her shoulder, and hugged her. Then Zoe stepped back, holding Catherine by the forearms, and stared into her eyes.

Zoe's heart plummeted. The centre of her mum's wide, blue irises were nothing but tiny, black pinpricks. Emitting a silent sigh, Zoe glanced around the room. It was clean and tidy. The polished timber floorboards gleamed. Plumped cushions stood to attention on the couch and the kitchen bench bore none of the usual empty wine bottles, glasses, and food scraps.

'Are you feeling better, Mum?'

'Darling! I'm wonderful. Adrian popped in this morning, and after he left, I gave the place a spring clean.'

Zoe groaned. They were back to square one.

She pushed past her mother and flung her schoolbag onto the floor in the corner of her bedroom. The lump in her stomach grew heavier.

'I thought we'd order pizza and watch a movie tonight. Just you and me—like old times,' Catherine called from the living room.

Zoe cleared her throat. 'Sure, Mum. I need to change my library books before they close.'

After stripping off her uniform, she threw on jeans and a T-shirt and shouldered her bag. 'I'll be back around five. We can order the pizza then, okay?'

Catherine didn't look up as she scrolled through her phone. 'Bye, darling. See you later.'

Zoe ran down the stairs, swinging savagely on the banister as she went. Her initial surge of hope wavered, as though held by a spider's thread, waiting to be swiped into oblivion. As she hurried along the road, she pressed curled knuckles against her mouth. She wanted to scream, yell, and cry like a toddler as vivid memories of the overheard conversation resurged. But what good would that do? Who could she tell? The police? If she did say something, would the big man or Adrian come after her? Fear gripped her as she approached the tiny park where, only a week earlier, she had been walking the same route and seen Adrian in a heated conversation with a much larger man. Not wanting to be recognised by Adrian, she had quickly stepped behind the hedge surrounding two sides of the park, out of sight, but not out of hearing.

'She's threatening to go to the cops. What should I do?' Adrian had mumbled.

'This will solve the problem,' the gravelly voice had answered.

Zoe had pressed closer into the hedge, peering through the leaves as the bigger man held up a clip-seal bag of white powder. Were they talking about her mother?

'I'm not going to do that.' Adrian's voice had trembled, his volume louder.

The man with the gravelly voice had spun Adrian around and held a knife to his neck.

'You are forgetting who is in charge here. You'll do as you're told. If you don't, no one will find your body.'

Adrian's terrified response had resounded in Zoe's ears as she had stealthily retreated to a side road and taken the longer route to the library, her jelly-like legs struggling to carry her.

Now, as she marched, Zoe pushed her fears to the back of her mind and forced her thoughts on her imag-

inary world—the one filled with purpose and appreciation. The one she was determined to achieve, even if
it took every waking moment to accomplish.

LATE SPRING in Brisbane was Zoe's favourite time of
year. The vibrant mauve flowers of the jacaranda trees
lined the streets and gardens, their petals brightening
the drab bitumen and detracting from the buzz and
chaos of the city. She stepped out of the library as a
light shower of rain fell, its gentle moisture generating
steam from the pavement. Zoe groped in her library
bag for the folding umbrella. Getting wet didn't worry
her but protecting books was an entirely different
matter.

Tilting her face upward, she breathed in the warm,
fresh air, revelling in the smell of rain. The shower
passed and she strode out, closing the umbrella and
glancing at the sky. She didn't wear a watch—hers had
broken long ago, and she hadn't liked to ask her
mother for money to buy a new one. The library clock
had shown four-thirty when she was checking out her
books, so she'd estimated she'd get home right on five
o'clock. A watery sun hovered low in the west. She gave
a small nod and increased her pace. She would be back
at the predicted time.

Furrows formed between her eyes as she turned

the corner into her street. Zoe flicked her long, dark hair from her face and stopped abruptly. Parked against the kerb fifty metres ahead was an ambulance, a police car, and a throng of spectators. Blue and red lights flashed, reflecting in the puddles.

For a second, her legs refused to work. Then she ran, terror growing inside her with every step.

Her life was about to change forever.

2

A shrill ring snapped Lola from dreamily gazing through the kitchen window, where the blue sky and the fresh spring air had gone almost unnoticed. She'd been dwelling on the long absence since her son's last visit. Lola wiped floured hands on her bright, floral apron and lifted the receiver to her ear.

'Hello. Featherwood Falls store—Lola speaking.'

'Mum. It's me. Ryan.'

A momentary leap of joy tore through her at the sound of his voice. Was he a mind-reader? He rarely phoned and when he did—except for the occasion of either her or Frank's birthday—the call was usually to advise of yet another change of employment, location, or even country.

'How are you, love? Where are you now?'

The line was silent for a few seconds, and Lola's breath hitched. Her intuition suggested whatever her son was about to tell her, it was going to be unexpected, possibly disappointing. She perched on a stool and leaned her elbows on the stainless-steel bench.

'I'm in Brisbane.'

Lola sat bolt upright again. *Really? Only hours away.* 'That's wonderful. Are you coming home?' Her voice quavered with hope.

'Yes. I've got a few things to sort out here first. Probably make it in about a week. How's Dad?'

'He's fine. Out delivering the mail. He'll be delighted to see you.'

Her mind raced. It had been years since their precious only child had been home. She would clear her sewing mess from his bedroom, bake his favourite fruit cake, and maybe buy some new towels to replace the worn pile in the linen cupboard.

With her thoughts wandering, she almost missed his next statement.

'I'll be bringing someone with me. Is that all right?'

'Of course, love. You know any friend of yours is welcome—always has been.' She smiled at the memories of hordes of school friends having sleepovers in years gone by. 'Is it one of your workmates ...' Excitement built inside her. 'Or is it a ... lady friend?'

Again, the silence stretched between them.

'Yes ... female. And she'll need her own room.' His

voice was hesitant, as though even he couldn't quite believe it.

'Don't worry, love. I'll have everything ready. How long do you think you'll be able to stay this time?' she finished brightly, crossing her fingers on the hand that rested on the bench.

'I really don't know. There's a lot I have to do here before we can come home—but I'll explain it all when we arrive.'

'Okay. I look forward to seeing you again—and of course, meeting your friend.'

'Righto. I've gotta go, Mum. I'll let you know when we'll be arriving.'

'That will be lovely. Bye now.'

'Bye.'

As she replaced the receiver, Lola returned to the kitchen window and stared. In her mind, Ryan was a child again, kicking a ball around with his friends or riding his horse with Emma in the paddock where the rescued kangaroos grazed.

Now a man in his early forties, he had roamed the world—worked in a variety of mines, oil rigs, and other isolated locations that prevented regular contact with friends and family. And it seemed he had a girl-friend. She was a little miffed that he had asked for a separate bedroom. These days, she presumed most couples, married or otherwise, shared a room—and a bed.

She sighed. Who was she to question? It would be a joy to wrap her arms around her son—and that was enough.

The shop bell rang, and Ginny Shepherd stepped through the doorway. 'Hi, Lola. I've run out of milk. Thought I'd pop in for a cuppa and a chat too—if you've got time?' She looked around the store. 'Not busy this morning?'

Lola smiled at her. Despite their age gap, she and Ginny had been close for decades—their friendship having deepened further over the past three years with the ongoing dramas that had plagued their small town. 'That would be lovely. I have news to share.'

'Oh. Sounds intriguing.' Ginny glanced at the rack of lamingtons on the table, their fresh chocolate-and-coconut coating dripping onto the surface beneath them. 'How about you get those into the fridge while I make the coffee?'

While the women sat at the small, round table in the café's corner, Lola regaled the substance of her telephone conversation with Ryan.

'That's brilliant news. I hope he can stay awhile. You'll have to come to the farm—Kirk and I'll put on a welcome-home barbeque for him.'

Lola brushed a lock of grey hair off her face, her dangling earrings swinging wildly as she turned to face the living quarters adjoining the back of the shop kitchen. 'I've got a bit of work to do. Ryan's room is a mess of sewing projects, and we've been using the spare room for storage.' Her voice rose. 'It's going to take some sorting.'

Ginny covered Lola's hand with her own. 'I'm here and can help. Why don't you talk to Frank when he gets home and decide where things can be put and then we can get started.'

Lola nodded. 'I can't believe it. Since the end of his and Emma's relationship, I've dreamt of Ryan bringing home a soulmate. Someone who can share his life when Frank and I are gone—and someone who might give us grandchildren.' Her face softened. 'We would love that.'

Ginny chuckled.

Anyone who walked around the back of the store would understand her need to share her love. Not only due to the many hand-reared kangaroos that hopped about, coming close to the fence at the sight of a human who might be generous enough to pat or feed them, but also the large, beautifully constructed row of wood-and-netted pens filled with recovering and orphaned koalas, possums, and other native animals. Getting up to feed tiny creatures every two or three hours in the night, coaxing traumatised baby animals to accept a rubber teat or eyedropper in order to obtain sustenance, and spending every spare dollar on special dietary requirements was a given for Lola. She did it because she could not bear to think every human and animal wasn't given a chance. Didn't they all deserve care and a purpose—even if survival was short-lived compared with humans?

'I understand, Lola.' Ginny stood and hugged the older woman. 'You have so much love in your heart. Any grandchildren you have—and remember, there's still time as Ryan's a relatively young man—will be the envy of many.'

Lola ducked her head, the heat in her cheeks deepening. 'That's enough of the babble, Ginny. I'd better make a start on tidying up while the shop's not busy.'

'I can stay,' Ginny repeated.

Lola flapped a hand. 'No, let me sort out what I can first, and I'll call you when I need help with the spare room.' She tapped a forefinger on her bottom lip. 'Pity I don't know what sort of woman she is. Should I buy a new doona cover?'

'Oh, Lola. I'm sure whatever the bedroom looks like, whoever she is will be happy. I'll help you clear it out, then we'll give it a good clean, put fresh sheets on the bed and a vase of flowers on the dresser.'

Meeting Ginny's smile with hers, Lola lowered her shoulders. 'You're right. Ryan's friends have always been polite and friendly. Why would this woman be any different?'

3

*B*ent over the piano, Emma closed her eyes, sinking into the rhythm of "Jessica's Theme" from the movie *The Man from Snowy River*. While her fingers flew, so too did memories—of her teenaged years when she and Ryan had ridden their horses up the valley, daring each other to canter close to the edge of the cliffs, imitating Jim Craig and Jessica Harrison. They had been blissfully happy days. Best friends for as long as she could remember, both had recently celebrated their fifteenth birthdays when their hormones ran rife, deepening their friendship into something that had both frightened and exhilarated her.

Opening her eyelids as her fingers quietened on the keys, she ended the piece with an emotional, heart-rending chord and lifted her gaze to the view. With the

French doors leading to the veranda flung wide, the gentle breeze wafted inside, lifting the delicate curtains that framed the scene beyond the piano. It was one she had never tired of. The neat, flower-filled garden against the white, picket fence provided a pretty foreground to the rolling, bush-clad hills that climbed to where moody, purple peaks and rugged crags took over, meeting the sky above.

It was easy to allow her mind to drift while soaking up the vista—to the days before love happened, before her mother's illness and Emma's life had turned upside down.

She took a deep breath and stretched her neck before closing the fallboard. How did it all go so wrong? What happened that November—her last month of high school? The one that sent her blissful life into a dark hole filled with misery and despair.

Not how, or what, but who?

A wren perched on the veranda rail, its dainty dance and pretty song disrupting Emma's reflections. Dragging herself back to the present, she heaved a sigh and glanced at the small, red kelpie lying in a patch of sunshine on the wooden boards.

'Come on, Piccolo. Let's go for a walk.'

The dog leapt to her feet and bounded to the back door, staring up at the lead hanging on a coat hook.

Emma chuckled, closed the veranda doors, then reached for the lead and clipped it on to the pup's collar. Her decision to purchase the puppy from Ginny and Claire Shepherd's latest litter had been a difficult one, particularly as her weekdays were filled with her teacher's aide role at the local school. It was Ashleigh, one of the teachers whose black-and-tan pup came from the same litter, who'd convinced Emma of the joy and company a dog could provide.

At three months of age, Piccolo was exuberant but already intensely devoted to Emma. Desperate to please, the little kelpie was also surprisingly obedient. Her recall still needed work, hence the extended length of thin rope tied to the end of the lead, but her manners—no jumping on people, sitting and dropping to her belly on command, and not eating until instructed—were progressing.

The biggest challenge for Emma was keeping up with Piccolo's energy. She hadn't realised how a kelpie's capacity to run fifty kilometres or more each day was entrenched in the breed. But she had witnessed enough troubled working dogs to understand their need for exercise of both mind and body. So, she rose an hour earlier than pre-dog-ownership and she and Piccolo walked and jogged along dirt tracks, up hills, and down valleys twice a day, gradually increasing the distance as the pup grew. Often, she would meet Ashleigh and her dog, who she had named Jazz, and the four of them would slow to a walk while letting the pups play together on their extended leads.

Emma's new routine had not only set Piccolo on the right path, but she was also feeling healthier and stronger than ever before. As she applied make-up and brushed her blonde hair into its immaculate bob each morning, the mirror reflected a glow she barely recognised—one that vaguely resembled the girl she had been eons ago, back when she was madly in love with Ryan and had an exciting future ahead of her.

IT WAS A HOT NOVEMBER SUNDAY, and the sun beat through Emma's hat, warming the top of her head, despite her watch face reading five o'clock.

'Let's walk, Piccolo. It's too hot to run.'

As they slowed their pace, Ashleigh and Jazz appeared from the end of the bush track two hundred metres ahead of Emma. She lifted an arm, and Ashleigh waved back.

The auburn-haired young woman Emma had grown fond of waited until she and Piccolo caught up to them, and they walked side-by-side toward the village.

'How's your weekend been?' Ashleigh asked.

'Pretty good. Quiet. Piccolo and I gardened this morning.' She laughed. 'Well, I pulled weeds out for a while until she got bored and dug a hole in my newly planted petunias. So, I gave up and took her for a walk. What about you?'

The glow on Ashleigh's face said it all. 'Damian and I went to Girraween for the weekend.'

'Oh. No Charlie?'

'No. He stayed home to "mind Dotty". We're kind of mixing things up now. Damian and I have time together without Charlie, then they have stints alone to do stuff they're used to—and then we have some outings together.'

Emma grinned at her friend. She was pleased the almost-six-year-old was more social. The intense, wildlife-obsessed little boy had taken a while to settle into school life. But following his insistence that too many local birds and reptiles had been disappearing without reason, and triggering Ashleigh's promise to establish why, their discovery of a smuggling ring in the area had shot the slightly antisocial boy to a position of revered importance with the other students. Emma was even more pleased for Damian and Ashleigh. Their slow-burning love-hate relationship had taken a positive turn since Claire and Rhys's engagement party, their shining glow of happiness encompassing everyone around them.

'Have you seen Lola and Frank this weekend?' Ashleigh asked.

Something in the younger woman's tone urged a rise in Emma's eyebrows. 'No. I popped in after school last week and picked up a few groceries but haven't been to the shop since. Why?'

'Their son is coming home next week. And he's bringing a lady friend with him.'

Emma's heart leapt before an icy chill ran down her back.

Ryan? It had been years since she'd caught sight of him from a distance, and even longer since they had exchanged any form of conversation. Could it be he had found love again? An ache welled deep inside her. Did she want to see him again?

No. Not if he's got a woman in his life.

4

*Z*oe slid a sideways glance at the man in the driver's seat. Large, work-roughened hands gripped the steering wheel, his fingers occasionally tapping along with the music pouring from the speakers.

He turned his head, catching her gaze before she had time to turn away. They'd been travelling for an hour, having left the city without a word spoken. He cleared his throat. 'Hard to comprehend really, isn't it?'

She gave a brief nod and focused on the road ahead of them.

'Did you think it strange your mother never told you?'

She shook her head, and seconds passed before she spoke. 'Not really. I wondered sometimes, especially when a man she called "a friend" started visiting.

But he turned out to be her dealer—not the father I had in mind,' she finished bitterly.

Another half hour passed before Zoe swallowed a mouthful from her water bottle and tentatively asked, 'How did you and Mum know each other?'

'We met when I was working in the mines in Western Australia. There'd been some legal issues on the worksite and Catherine was part of the investigation team.' He turned to face Zoe, his blue eyes edged with creases and the sides of his mouth down-turned, giving him a sad, hangdog appearance.

Zoe stifled an unexpected chortle as he continued.

'It was a long time ago ...'

'Yeah—like, nearly seventeen years, obviously.'

'You're right. It was. So, it's hazy, and I'm sorry if I came across negatively.' He shook his head. 'Our relationship was brief, and I guess we both accepted it as nothing more than a fling. But I am surprised she never told me she was pregnant.' Heaving a sigh, he added, 'If I'd known, I would have been there for you, Zoe.'

Waves of anger and disbelief rolled through her at unpredictable intervals. She hadn't been the one to insist on having the DNA tests done. He had—and she didn't blame him.

Shrugging, she released a long breath. 'Guess it was as much of a shock for you as for me.'

'Yep. Sure was.' He smiled at her then—a wide grin that reached his eyes and lit up his face.

For a brief second, a wobbly smile touched her lips. They had known one another only a few days, but from the moment of introduction, she had experienced a wary sense of relief, of hope, and the hint of an emotional bond that inextricably linked the two of them. 'What do you do?'

Ryan glanced at her with eyebrows raised.

'At the mine, I mean.' She rushed on. 'Like, do you drive one of those gigantic trucks or a dragline?'

'Neither. I'm a mechanical engineer. It's my job—along with a few others—to keep the machinery running.'

'Oh.'

With measured hesitation, as though afraid of boring her, Ryan elaborated on his position—the positives and negatives of multinational mining companies taking him to all corners of the world, and the two investment properties he had purchased over the years with the above-average salary.

'Where?' Zoe asked.

'One in Yeppoon and one in Blackwater. Both have tenants in them, but one day ...' His mouth twisted as he took a deep breath. 'Maybe I'll sell them to buy a farm or business and get out of mining altogether.'

Neither raised the subject of Catherine's death—or her life.

AFTER THEIR STOP in Warwick for lunch, Zoe tapped her phone furiously, her heart sinking as the service bars dropped from three to one and then greyed out completely. Swathes of farmland and native bush flashed past as she lost connectivity with Amy and Natalia. Even the smells in the air had changed. Gone was the hustle of the city. When she rolled her window down, the breeze held nothing but the scent of manure, eucalyptus, and swarms of flies.

'No service?' Ryan asked.

'Nothing!' She slammed her phone down on her knee.

'Hey. Don't stress. Once we get close to each town, it'll come back. Anyway, your grandparents have wi-fi at the shop now and there's apparently a new phone tower just up the road, so you should be able to connect and message all you like.'

She shuffled in her seat, fighting the nausea churning inside her. What would they be like? How long would she be expected to stay out in this godforsaken place? She was a city girl. With two high school years still in front of her—and then, she hoped, another four at university—she needed the best education she could get to study medicine. Living in Woop-Woop land definitely didn't feature on her agenda. She was sixteen. Legally, she could do as she pleased.

Swallowing her frustration, she stared through the window. That was the trouble. While she didn't legally have to live with a parent, what other choices did she have? Foster homes, sleezy shared accommodation with unruly youths who would likely steal the shirt off her back—amongst other much worse things—or join the homeless and sleep under bridges or in the park. No, there was no way she was going down that road. If only her stupid mother had fought her addiction and not been dismissed from her well-paid career as a solicitor. She was a smart woman. So why had she succumbed to the life of a druggy? The social worker had hinted it may have been due to her work being so stressful that she'd turned to anything to help her get through the busy days. Zoe didn't know—and now, as sorrow and anger consumed her, she didn't care. The person she loved most in her life had let her down and she couldn't forgive her—not at the moment, anyway.

The empty ache of hopelessness had consumed her as she and the social worker sat in the office, facing the kind but professional face of her mother's ex-supervisor. Shocked to hear there was nothing left in the bank, icy panic had run through her veins. Every dollar had been spent, leaving an unpaid mortgage and a mountain of bills. Catherine's superannuation would not be available to Zoe until she reached the age of twenty-five—and by the time they sold the apartment, there would be just enough to cover outstanding debts.

She shot a glance at Ryan again. Her father. There was no other choice but to hope her instincts didn't fail her and trust he'd fulfill his promise of providing for her, at least until she was in a financial position to take care of herself. But living hours away from friends and all she knew filled her with overwhelming grief.

5

*F*rank threw the door open. 'Lola. They're here!'

She wiped her hands on a towel, brushed the wayward strands of hair off her face, and hustled toward the shop's front door, her heart thumping.

A white Toyota Prado was parked beside the store, midway between the shop entrance and the gate leading to the attached-living area behind it. Ryan stepped onto the road and strode around to the passenger side as Lola and Frank approached. Before he had a chance to assist, the door opened, revealing a skinny, denim-clad leg. Ryan faced his parents—the passenger hidden by his bulk.

With outstretched arms, Lola rushed to him and pressed herself against the tall, muscled frame of her son, holding him tightly for a few seconds.

After gently prising himself free of his mother's embrace, Ryan hugged his father and met his parents' beaming smiles with a wavering grin. Stepping back, he then beckoned the fragile teenager standing beside the car.

She inched slowly toward him, her arms folded against her chest.

'Mum, Dad. This is Zoe, my daughter.'

A bolt of shock zapped through Lola, and for a second she wobbled. Had her hearing failed and her dreams overwhelmed reality?

Blinking away the surprise, she stepped forward, clasped Zoe's hand between her palms, and leaned to kiss her cheek. 'How wonderful to meet you. Welcome to Featherwood Falls.'

Frank stood stock-still, his jaw sagging and his eyes wide. 'I-I,' he stuttered. 'I didn't know you had a daughter?'

Ryan shot Zoe a gentle smile. 'Neither did I until a few days ago.'

Zoe studied the ground and shuffled a sneaker-clad foot in the loose gravel.

'Come on then. Let's get you out of this sun and you can tell us all about it. I imagine you're hungry and thirsty after your drive.' Lola led the way through the side gate, past the army of pansies lining the house wall, and into the open kitchen and living area.

The shop bell rang as she put the kettle on.

'I'll get it,' Frank said as he hurried past, his aging frame stooped under the thatch of white hair.

Lola bustled around, placing glasses, home-made lemonade, lamingtons, and sausage rolls on the dining table. She was desperate to think of the right thing to say but instead said nothing.

They sat down as Frank returned, and Lola found her voice.

'I'm terribly sorry, Zoe. You must think we've got no social skills. We're delighted to meet you—although it's taking a little time to get used to the idea of Frank and me having a grandchild.' She smiled at Zoe, who responded with a solemn-faced stare.

Lola cleared her throat and turned to her son, silently begging him to fill in the gaps.

After polishing off two sausage rolls and a glass of lemonade, he began. 'I received a phone call about Zoe a couple of weeks ago. Zoe's mum passed away suddenly, leaving her with a neighbour while the solicitor and social workers sorted out the estate. Catherine had registered my name as Zoe's father on the birth certificate, but they had to locate me. Apparently, there are a lot of Ryan Browns in Australia, so that took a while. Then, because neither Zoe nor I believed it, we both had DNA tests.' He paused and shot Zoe a sheepish smile. 'Luckily for Zoe, she looks like her mum and not me.'

Lola pressed her hands against her cheeks. 'You

poor girl. I'm so sorry for your loss—and for not being there for you all these years. If only we'd known.'

Zoe shrugged, her head bowed as she stared at the phone in her lap. 'Can I log on to your wi-fi?' she said, looking up.

Zoe's question startled Lola as much as the girl's deep turquoise eyes did. It was the first time she had spoken, her voice soft and polite but determined.

She held her gaze while Lola pushed herself to her feet and walked to the fridge, where she peeled off a magnetic, pink card and handed it to Zoe with a smile. 'Here you go. Sorry, love, I should have thought about it earlier. I know how you young ones live on your phone.'

Their eyes met again, and Zoe gave the slightest nod, her lips quirking a little. 'Thanks.'

Lola's empathy blossomed. The girl had finished her drink but had barely nibbled the end of her sausage roll. *You must be missing your mum—and your friends dreadfully.* She rested a gentle hand on her shoulder.

'When you're logged into the wi-fi, would you like to come and see your room?' She glanced at Ryan. 'Bring Zoe's belongings in please, dear. I'm sure she would like to unpack.' Lola had no idea what Zoe would like to do, but she suspected messaging her friends would take priority over unpacking.

Sliding a quick look at the thin, sad girl again,

Lola's heart lurched. With long, dark hair and a clear, unblemished complexion, Zoe was beautiful in her fragility.

Sucking in a slow, deep breath, Lola lowered her shoulders. No doubt she was about to embark on a big learning curve in teenage management. But Zoe was her own flesh and blood, and Lola would ensure she received the care and love she deserved—no matter how hard that road might be.

THE MURMUR of male voices continued through the afternoon while a steady stream of customers kept Lola busy in the shop. Worried about Zoe and desperate to find out more from Ryan, Lola couldn't wait for closing time. When six o'clock arrived, she nipped through the adjoining door into the post office, flicked the deadlock on the solid timber entry, then returned to the store and flipped over the *Closed* sign.

Reassuring herself Frank would do another security check before darkness fell, she retreated to the comfortable home attached to the rear of the building, pausing to check the chicken in the fridge had completely thawed.

Ryan looked up as she entered the living room.

'Where's Zoe?' Lola spun her gaze around the room, her brow furrowing.

'Gone for a walk,' Ryan answered.

Lola sucked in a sharp breath. 'Is she all right? The poor girl's only been here five minutes. She doesn't know her way around.'

'It's okay, Mum. Zoe is far more worldly than any of us would have been at that age. She needs to stretch her legs and look around, and she'll be perfectly safe.' He snorted a suppressed laugh. 'Featherwood Falls is not exactly a thriving metropolis. She can't get lost.'

'Hmm. I hope you're right.' Except for Briony and Claire Shepherd, she had been too busy to get to know many teenagers since Ryan passed through that awkward age on his way to adulthood. The Shepherd girls' mutual love of animals had solidified a close, caring relationship with both Frank and her as they grew, treating them with the reciprocal love and respect of grandparents. She sank into the armchair, hoping that she and Zoe might have a similar relation-ship—eventually.

Meeting her son's amused expression, she said, 'You'd better tell us what we need to know—like how long you are staying and how you are going to look after Zoe and continue working at the same time?'

'We've just been talking about that, love.' Frank shuffled to the edge of his chair and leaned forward, his voice dropping to barely more than a whisper. 'Zoe will be with us for more than a few days.'

With eyebrows raised, Lola faced her son.

'Yeah. Sorry, Mum.' Ryan turned his hands palms up and shrugged. 'Two weeks ago, I wasn't a parent as far as I knew. Now I'm the father of a sixteen-year-old daughter thanks to a brief liaison with Catherine when I was working in Western Australia. She never contacted me again, and I had no idea she was pregnant.' He squirmed as though divulging anything to do with his sex life to his parents was taboo. 'I didn't know what else to do.'

Lola straightened, her face soft. 'I understand, son. It's as much of a shock to you as to us ... the question is, how do we manage the situation for everyone's benefit? She's a broken young girl who's just lost her mother. She doesn't know any of us, and we need to keep her safe and ensure she knows she's welcome in our family.'

Ryan nodded then leaned his head into his hands, kneading his forehead fiercely as if it was a lump of dough. Straightening, he said, 'I've only got one two-week swing left on the current job. After that, I had planned to have a holiday break before I started a new contract in New Guinea. To be honest, after all that's happened these past few days, I can't see any other option but to cancel all arrangements except Zoe's care.'

He sat back and glanced at Frank and then Lola. 'Term finishes in a couple of weeks, and I've already spoken to Zoe's school. Fortunately, exams are over, and the principal said Zoe wouldn't be forfeiting anything if she was to finish now—except the end-of-year social stuff, which I think she's lost interest in anyway. So ... I was thinking she could stay here while I work my last shift block, then I'll come back and we can have Christmas and January together, getting to know one another and making plans for the future.' His face slackened with exhaustion, creases shadowing the hope in his eyes.

Lola met Frank's stare, and he gave her an approving nod.

'That's a sensible plan. How about you help feed the animals, Ryan?' Frank said. 'Then, if Zoe hasn't returned by the time we finish, you can find her.'

She retreated to the kitchen and opened the fridge door before staring blankly at its contents. Out of habit, she reached for the lettuce as a warm flush of hope and something more—excitement?—enveloped her.

Our son is home, and we have a granddaughter!

She was in unknown territory. A mix of both delight and trepidation swirled through Lola.

6

*A*fter texting back and forth with Amy, Natalia, and Mrs Worth—advising them of her arrival in Featherwood Falls and ending with, "Tell you more when I've checked out the place"—Zoe wandered along the main road and crossed the bridge. She paused to lean over the railing, mesmerised by the gentle hiss and slap of the water tumbling over rocks. The numbness inside her eased, her attention switching to the unfamiliar noises of the country— bird calls she hadn't heard before, the bellows of cows and bleats of sheep. The muted hum of a tractor in the distance reached her as it chugged in circles around a paddock. After continuing her walk to the end of the village, she paused at a side road where the speed sign read *100*.

Then, turning back, she ambled toward the town

again and swung up a narrow bitumen road where the broken edges crumbled, mingling with roughly mown grass. A dozen houses straggled along the hillside overlooking the river, their extensive gardens dotted with shady trees and their windows glistening in the afternoon sun.

Since the moment she had reached the crowd outside their Brisbane house and Mrs Worth enveloped her in a teary hug, she had felt nothing. Obviously expecting her to burst into tears, Mrs Worth had pressed a handkerchief into her palm and, with a tight grip around her, had guided Zoe through the plethora of uniformed police and paramedics until they'd reached the sanctuary of her neighbour's apartment. Explaining she had popped over with a cake and had been surprised to find the door unlocked, Mrs Worth said she had called and when no one answered, she had gone in to leave the baking on the bench. That was when she'd found Catherine lying on the lounge-room floor.

Police and social workers had come and gone, each questioning Zoe gently and issuing murmured sympathy as they'd attempted to prise the facts from her. When the police asked her where Catherine had obtained the drugs from, Zoe had shaken her head— consumed with fear as the incident in the park between Adrian and the large man remained forefront in her mind. Zoe kicked a piece of broken concrete and it clattered into a patch of dry weeds. Her mother had gone, and nothing could change that. To mention Adrian or the conversation she had witnessed would only complicate her life. She was on her own now and had to take care of herself. Mrs Worth had defended both Zoe and Catherine as fiercely as a dog defending her pups, and eventually the police agreed to wait until the forensic and toxicology reports had been released before they talked to her again.

With each step along the dusty road, Zoe tingled. It was as though she had drowned, but new life was being breathed into her. The empty, emotionless state of shock was morphing into something else—something all-consuming. The summer breeze wafted over her, stroking away loneliness and desolation with a gentle hand. Her steps grew firmer and more determined. She leaned forward as a spear of anger took her by surprise, shooting through her and biting at the cavity that had once been filled with love and happiness—before she had glimpsed the pale, blue-lipped face of her mother.

I should never have left her! She raged at herself. Catherine had overdosed before. It had become more frequent in the past few months. Only, on each of those occasions, she had recovered—thanks to the close watch Mrs Worth kept on both Zoe and her mother.

Zoe frowned. How had Mrs Worth known? The

stern-faced woman in her seventies had been like a pseudo-grandmother to Zoe from the day they'd moved in—sitting with her while she did her homework and waiting for her mother to return from work, popping in at regular intervals with delicious meals and baking because she "loved to cook". A retired teacher, for almost five years, she had been Zoe's guardian angel and a firm friend, despite keeping her own story to herself. Zoe had asked her once if she had children, and she'd pressed her thin lips together and shaken her head. The subject hadn't been mentioned again though they'd gone on to share their compassion for Catherine and a mutual, poor opinion of Adrian.

Clenching her fist as anger rolled over her once more, a vision of the sly, narrow-faced junky who'd frequented their home flashed through Zoe's head. His visits had coincided perfectly with Catherine's depression, and Zoe had been helpless to stop her. The hits had left Catherine swinging between fabulous highs that had her buzzing for days, achieving goals and processing mountains of work in a flash, to extreme lows where she dragged herself from her bed to the bathroom and lay, sick and frail, on the tiled floor.

Stomping furiously along the roadside, the fire in Zoe's head swirled with increasingly hot anger as she reflected on the number of times she had had to clean her mother up, help her shower, and put her to bed. *It should have been the other way around.*

Spotting a dirt track leading uphill toward the bush, Zoe noted the loosely wired fence at the end of the road, separating the track from a grassy paddock where a handful of sheep grazed. After hesitating for only a moment, she cast a quick glance around and slipped through the road gate. She hurried across the paddock and squeezed between the poorly maintained wooden rails, glancing fearfully behind her in case the sheep gave chase. The hint of a grin touched her face as only two of the animals had raised their heads to look at her while the others continued grazing.

She climbed higher and turned to look back on the village. Although a city dweller, in happier days she and her mother had regularly walked around Brisbane's Botanic Gardens and the parks that dotted the city. The vista in front of her bore no similarities. The sheer magnitude of the surrounding hills, native bush, and neat farms that encompassed the tiny town took her by surprise.

'It's quite pretty, really,' she whispered aloud.

While she stood soaking in the scene and attempting to control the anger that still burned within her, the faint sound of piano music floated in the air. She turned her head slightly to pinpoint its origin. At the end of the last road of dwellings below stood a small cottage similar to the historic houses of Spring Hill and pockets of the inner-city suburbs she was familiar with. The surrounding lush gardens and lawn reached to touch sheep-and-cow-filled paddocks. Her gaze swept toward the vaguely familiar road that had led her and her father to the town of Featherwood Falls. She narrowed her eyes, getting her bearings and making out the general store with Ryan's car parked outside. They were closer than she'd thought—a paddock dotted with what appeared to be kangaroos linking the back of the store with the fields below her and a wide strip of bitumen highlighting the main road.

The music reached her again, and she breathed deeply, wrestling with the diminishing threads of anger every time she thought of her mother. Treading carefully back down the track, her eyes and ears focused on the cottage from which she was certain the music was coming. A white-picket fence encompassed a brightly coloured garden, with a row of shrubs edging the paddock outside the fence.

As Zoe drew closer, the melody of "The Climb", one of Miley Cyrus's songs and a favourite of her own, became recognisable. Compelled, she crept closer to the fence and leaned on it before closing her eyes and silently mouthing the words.

The music ended, and she remained where she was for a few moments, letting memories of happy days singing in the school choir fill her soul.

'Are you alright?'

Zoe jerked to attention and her eyelids fluttered

open. She faced the concerned expression of a woman around her own mother's age standing on the veranda of the cottage. Only this lady had neatly groomed blonde hair and a small, rust-coloured dog at her feet.

Zoe nodded. 'I-I'm fine. Just listening to the music.'

The woman's face softened and an understanding smile that exuded warmth and compassion spread across her face. 'That's nice. It's one of my favourite pieces.'

'Mine too.'

'I don't think I've seen you around. Home from school for the holidays?'

Zoe shook her head, suddenly overwhelmed with the urge to get away. She didn't want to talk to anyone. Returning to the store and shutting herself in the bedroom became her goal.

Lifting her hand in a brief wave, she broke into a jog, catching the bewildered frown of the blonde woman out of the corner of her eye as she bolted down the road.

A sob broke from her throat as she ran. It was as though she was two people. One who wasn't ready to be thrown into the unknown. Who wanted to curl up in a corner and weep for all she had lost, all the questions that hadn't been answered, and for her dreams of the future. The other Zoe tried to ignore the hint of promise that fluttered inside her, giving thanks to people who, at this point anyway, had welcomed her kindly and offered her a new beginning.

A sliver of anger weighed on the seesaw of her mind again, and she grunted. *What am I doing in this tin-pot town?*

Ryan appeared in front of her, as though her thoughts had conjured him up, marching along the road with the worried, kind, hangdog expression that she recognised as concern. It brought a lump to her throat.

He smiled as she drew close, turned, and fell into step beside her.

They walked toward the store.

'Have a good look around?' he asked.

She sighed heavily and shrugged. 'S'pose so.'

'I understand, Zoe. It's tough for us both. But now I'm getting used to the idea of having a daughter, I'm pretty excited.' He looked down at her and shared a lopsided grin.

For the first time in weeks, hope wormed its way inside her. Perhaps things wouldn't be too bad. After all, she would no longer have to hide her mother's failings ... and she had a father and two grandparents who'd seemed happy to meet her and include her in their lives, even if it had been a shock to them all. That was pretty cool.

She nodded and quickened her step.

THROUGHOUT DINNER, Zoe barely said a word but when the bundle in the wicker basket moved and the tiny face of a joey popped out, Zoe's solemn, deadpan expression changed to one of delighted surprise. Lola prepared a miniature bottle of formula and sat beside Zoe, smiling as the baby kangaroo nuzzled the teat and began sucking.

'Would you like to feed her?' Lola asked. 'I call her Pixie.'

Zoe's hesitant smile widened as she reached over, and together they gently settled the bundle on Zoe's lap. With the bottle empty, Lola showed Zoe how to toilet the little creature and tuck her back into the cosy bag. Empathy flowed from the girl as she slowly opened up, asking questions about how and where the joey had been found. While Frank and Ryan cleared the dishes and washed up, Lola took Zoe on a stealthy, torch-lit walk around the pens and paddock behind the house. As she pointed out the koala that had been hit by a car but had healed nicely and was almost ready for release, the aviary with a magpie nursing a broken wing, and the weaned, older kangaroos and wallabies that were free to return to the bush but showed a reluctance to do so, Zoe's interest grew. Like a flower opening to the morning sun, Zoe began to talk, sharing her dreams of joining the medical fraternity once she had finished school. Zoe's silent reserve morphed to an animated and interested teenager showing a reluctance to return inside and generating a delighted smile from her grandmother. After joining the others in an after-dinner cup of tea, Zoe excused herself, spent an extraordinarily long time in the bathroom, and disappeared into her bedroom.

HOURS LATER, Zoe lay in the old room, staring at the dark shadow in the corner. The wooden dressing table, its drawers lined with lavender-scented paper, contained her meagre pile of clothes. A vase of sweet-smelling roses rested in front of the mirror on a lace doily. She mulled over the sudden changes in her life, vaguely resting her gaze on the outline of old pictures hanging on the walls that appeared only as texts from friends lit up the room. Were they her relatives? One photo could have been a young Lola and Frank with Ryan between them—a smiling, blond-haired boy in a T-shirt and shorts with a ninja-turtle cape around his shoulders. Tomorrow she would ask Lola.

Her stomach churned, struggling to digest the too-large dinner she had consumed. Her body was tired but restless, unable to settle. Outside, a bird called—a mournful sound unfamiliar to her. An owl perhaps?

She rolled over, pressing her face into the pillow, the fragrance of citrus laundry powder filling her nostrils.

So, this was her home—for now. Was this going to be the new normal for her? She took a deep breath and squeezed her eyes tight, willing sleep to come.

Nothing was normal anymore.

---

7

*E*mma's brow furrowed as the girl jogged down the road. She was familiar with most families in the town, but country life had increased in popularity since the pandemic. Many occupations were now achievable online and, consequently, Featherwood Falls was growing.

While she knew all the primary school children, teenagers were different. Some went to Toowoomba or Brisbane to one of the popular boarding facilities, while the balance of locals were bussed into Warwick for their high-school years before leaving school and—most times—the area.

She took a deep breath. The sun hung low in the western sky, its glow tinting the paddocks with gold. Emma smiled at Piccolo.

'Let's go for a walk.'

Minutes later, she strode along the track leading to the hills, Piccolo trotting on a long leash in front of her, her mind still on the girl. There had been something about the slightly built teenager—a quiet determination that didn't fit the frail figure. She had seemed jumpy, afraid. Or had it been something more?

Emma's mind wandered to the assignment she had finished the evening before, the final submission in her course. Although deciding long ago to forgo her dreams of teaching—she was comfortable on her salary and didn't envy Quinn or Ashleigh's workload when it came to preparation, reporting, and conducting parent/teacher interviews—she enjoyed the extra stimulation of studying human behaviour and social science. It helped her recognise children who were struggling with issues that were other than academic. The dark-haired girl remained firmly fixed in her mind. A sadness had seemed to hang over her. Perhaps she had broken up with a boyfriend. Or her parents were going through a tough time.

Piccolo jerked on the leash as a hare shot out from beneath a log and the pup attempted to follow it. Emma grasped the loop around her wrist with the other hand, reeling the dog toward her as she spoke sternly. 'No!'

Piccolo wagged her tail furiously but returned to Emma with reluctant obedience.

Taking a firmer grip on the lead, Emma increased

her pace. 'Come on then, we'll run for a while. That should wear you out.'

Ten minutes later, they paused for a rest and Emma leaned forward, panting, her hands on her knees.

She glanced around, surprised to have subconsciously chosen that exact spot to stop. They stood in a small clearing where the track edged the path. Directly opposite, flanked by dark green ranges and jagged outcrops, was the escarpment where she and Ryan had ridden their horses many years earlier. Although she often walked this way, she mostly averted her eyes and fought any memories threatening to surge. This time, though, those reminiscences had a mind of their own, forcing her to draw a shuddering breath while they consumed her once again.

Despite the passing years, "that" night remained entrenched in her mind and soul. One minute she and Ryan had been entwined in a tight embrace at the end-of-year school ball, their mutual love of music and dancing locking them together as one. The next, someone had tapped on her shoulder to advise her mother, Maureen, had been rushed to hospital. A stroke, they'd said. With no recollection of how she got there, or how long she'd stayed by her mother's side, Emma remembered only the anguish when, days later, the doctors had advised Maureen would need care for the rest of her life. Plans to move to Toowoomba with Ryan—she was going to study teaching while he pursued his interest in engineering—

melted like ice cream on a tropical summer's day. Months later, there had just been the two of them. Mother and daughter. To add to Emma's devastation, Ryan's outstanding exam results had secured him a place at The University of Queensland in Brisbane—a more than three-hour drive away but one that might as well have been on the other side of the world.

Why didn't he come and see me? We agreed we would stick together through anything that came our way. Friends for life—and a little bit more.

Piccolo yipped, and Emma's attention sprang back to the present. Emma had lost the enthusiasm for walking and long shadows now stretched across the path as the sun sank.

'Sorry, girl. We'll have a longer walk in the morning. Let's go home and get you some dinner.'

BACK IN HER COTTAGE, Emma shook the bag of kibble, peering into the packet as if hoping her gaze would magically multiply the few remaining crumbs.

'Darn it. I forgot to get more for you the other day. How about I cook you vegetables and rice—and while I do that, you can have a brisket bone?'

Piccolo turned her head on one side and then the other, as though absorbing and understanding every word Emma said. Her tongue lolled and she moved to the back door while Emma dug in the freezer, extracted the bone, and followed the pup outside. Piccolo sat without command and waited until Emma placed it on a patch of fresh, green lawn and gave the routine hand signal. As the dog plonked herself in front of the treat and began chewing, Emma returned to the kitchen and chopped up vegetables.

The thought of having to go to the store the following day brought a tightness to Emma's throat. Would she bump into Ryan? Or worse. Would she meet his girlfriend in the shop? Perhaps they were helping Lola and Frank and might be staying longer than just the weekend. Despite her attempt to control her memories, they returned once again. And for the umpteenth time, she wondered what her life would have been if her father had survived the farming accident when she was three and her mother had not had a stroke.

AFTER SCHOOL THE FOLLOWING DAY, Emma sucked in a deep breath, lowered her shoulders, and stepped through the door as the bell tinkled above her.

The shop was empty except for the mother of one of last year's graduates from Featherwood Falls

Primary School and a relatively new resident of the town.

'Hello, Emma. How are you?'

Emma smiled at the bubbly, golden-haired woman, searching the depths of her memory for a name. Jennifer? Janet? Yes, that was it. 'Fine thanks. You?'

'I'm great—especially now Lola's giving me a few hours a week to help here. I don't know how that woman has carried on alone for so long.' She glanced around the shop. 'It's quiet at the moment but you know how busy it can get, especially now she's got this state-of-the-art coffee machine. It draws the customers in like a magnet.'

Emma's tumbling stomach settled as she registered this information. 'That's good to hear. I'm sure Lola and Frank are grateful for your help.' A quick look at the adjoining door between the shop and post office confirmed there was no sign of anyone else in there either. She hastened to the corner where the shelves and a small fridge contained an array of dog and cat food, snatched up a bag of kibble with a picture of a puppy on the front, and placed it on the counter.

'That's all today?' Janet asked.

'Yes, thank you.' She had no intention of sharing her fears of running into Ryan—or the woman he had brought home—and wanted to reach her cottage as quickly as possible.

After tapping her card on the machine, she smiled

her thanks and hurried out the door. An unfamiliar car drove past and a group of children played on the trampoline in the front yard of a house a few doors away. They waved cheerily, and she returned the wave before turning into the shortcut that led across the paddock to her cottage, her thumping pulse slowing with every step.

After dumping the bag of dog food on the bench, she met Piccolo's interested stare and reached out to pat her.

'Yep. That's for you, and no, I didn't see Ryan—or any of the Brown family.'

Piccolo thumped her tail on the floor, nudging Emma's hand as she gazed with adoring eyes.

Emma's breathing returned to normal, and relief flowed through her as she slumped into a chair. But, despite the release of apprehension at the thought of running into Ryan and his lady friend, somewhere deep inside her, a sliver of disappointment gnawed.

8

*L*ola snatched her apron from the hook on the back of the kitchen door and pushed up her sleeves before taking the tray of sponge cake from the oven. *Next job—cut and ice the lamingtons.*

She had gotten through the first few sleepless nights of knowing she was a grandparent and cautious anticipation bubbled. While lying awake in the small hours, listening to Frank's gentle snores beside her, she'd replayed the first evening's events after Zoe's arrival over and over in her mind.

At least she had good manners. Zoe's mother—or someone—had obviously provided a good example.

Lola had risen early and baked a fresh batch of lamingtons and pies before the shop opened, then rang Janet, the young woman recently employed as a casual assistant, confirming her availability to work in the shop before accepting Ginny Shepherd's offer of an afternoon at the farm. Having grown up in the country, animals had always been a constant in her life, and now with the softening of Zoe's attitude and the intrigue the girl had shown with the animals and birds, Lola was sure a trip to Featherwood Station would be a successful one—especially as Claire would be there. Although several years apart in age, Claire's quiet, compassionate nature would provide the closest thing to a friend that Zoe might find before returning to school.

At least, Lola hoped so.

As USUAL, Frank left at seven-thirty to begin the mail run. And on the third day following their arrival, instead of the usual hour or more before either Ryan or Zoe emerged that allowed Lola to complete her outside chores, Zoe staggered from her bedroom early to join Ryan who was slumped in a lounge chair yawning and rubbing his eyes.

Surprised, but secretly pleased at the change in routine, Lola bustled around the table, setting out plates and bowls of fruit salad and yoghurt for them. She and Frank had eaten two hours earlier—a routine they had held for decades.

'Tea? Coffee?' Lola asked. 'Would you like cereal,

bacon and eggs, or toast for breakfast today—or all of them?' She grinned, her silver hair wafting wildly around her glowing cheeks as she met each of the sleepy faces.

Zoe glanced at her father.

He smiled at them both. 'Thanks, Mum. You know me. I'll have everything. What about you, Zoe?'

She met Lola's eyes before tilting her head at the food on the table. 'I'm happy with fruit and yoghurt ... and a piece of toast.' Hesitating for only a moment, she stepped past Lola and flicked her hair over her shoulder. 'I can get it, though. I'm used to looking after myself.'

Lola nodded, swallowing a wave of compassion. *Of course you are.*

The morning passed quickly as, replete with the huge breakfast, Ryan served in the shop while Lola accepted Zoe's offer of help to ice the lamingtons. With two large trays of the delicious chocolate-and-coconut-coated sponge cakes cooling in the fridge, Lola bit back surprise when Zoe asked, 'Would you let me help with the animals? I'd like to learn.'

'Of course, love. Frank and I usually do the morning rounds before our business day begins, but I can show you more now if you like? If you don't mind getting up a bit earlier, you can help tomorrow.'

They walked around the pens, checked the water containers, and added another branch of eucalyptus leaves to the koala's pen before Lola pointed to the open gate at the far side of the enclosure separating the bushland from the paddock. 'We close that each night to prevent predators from coming in, then open it in the morning so the kangaroos can go into the bush to graze.'

One of the remaining kangaroos hopped over to Zoe, and she startled, pressing close to Lola's side.

'Don't be afraid, Zoe. This is Wattle. She's very gentle, and although she has her own joey in her pouch now, she insists on coming home each night.' Lola chuckled. 'Why wouldn't you? The food is guaranteed, and you get to sleep without having to worry about predators.' Lola rubbed the kangaroo's chest as she spoke, while Wattle clutched Lola's hand with her two front paws. 'See? She wants a pat and won't hurt you.'

Tentatively, Zoe reached out and stroked the kangaroo's chest exactly as Lola had.

A smile spread over her face as the kangaroo hopped away to follow another into the bush. 'They're beautiful,' she breathed. 'I've never seen one up close. Only on television—although I remember Mum taking me to Lone Pine Koala Sanctuary once when I was little.' She shrugged and gave Lola a wry grin. 'I was frightened of them then 'cause they seemed huge.'

Lola smiled.

'Why don't you have a dog?' Zoe asked.

'We did. Poor old Boris passed over the rainbow bridge about eight weeks ago. That's his grave over there.' She pointed to a white-painted cross in the paddock's corner under a eucalyptus tree.

'Oh. How old is "old" for a dog?'

'Boris was sixteen. That's a fairly good age for most dogs. Some don't even make it into double figures.'

'That's sad.' Zoe's gaze turned back to the kangaroos.

'Perhaps you could consider studying to be a veterinarian instead of a doctor,' Lola suggested with a grin. 'Animals might not tell you where it hurts, but they're very rewarding to work with.'

Zoe said nothing, but it was clear from her growing interest that a whole new train of thought had opened for her granddaughter. An interest they shared.

AFTER HALF-EXPECTING DISINTEREST FROM ZOE, who had spent the rest of the morning shut in her room—presumably texting her friends—Lola was pleasantly surprised by the girl's willingness to join the two septuagenarians and a father she'd only known for two weeks for the afternoon. Zoe had slipped her phone into her pocket, picked up the container of lamingtons, and was first to reach the car.

As usual, they were greeted by a cacophony of

barking as they climbed out of the vehicle at the Featherwood Station homestead.

Lola followed Zoe's gaze to where the sound was coming from. 'It's okay. We're not about to have a pack of dogs launch on us. They're in kennels and well controlled.'

'Hi there!'

A cheery voice called, and everyone turned toward the middle-aged woman with shoulder-length brown hair.

The woman hugged Lola and Frank before Lola introduced Zoe. Ginny greeted their granddaughter with a smile. Behind her, a tall, thin young woman appeared and gave Lola and Frank a hug before facing Ryan and Zoe.

She extended her hand to Zoe, who took it hesitantly.

'Hi. I'm Claire.' Turning to Ryan, she grinned. 'I know we've met before, but I'm sorry—it's been so long I hardly remember you.'

'I understand. You've changed a bit since I last saw you, too.' He raised his eyebrows and looked down, holding his hand at thigh level horizontally. 'I think you were about this big.'

They all laughed, and Claire retorted, 'Probably. The years have a way of changing us all, don't they?'

'Come in. Claire's got the kettle on.' Ginny shot Zoe

a warm smile. 'It's lovely to meet you, Zoe. I hope you'll be happy in Featherwood Falls.'

Lola glimpsed surprised confusion in Zoe's eyes, and her heart squeezed. *Early days. Don't push.*

As though instantly realising she had said too much, Ginny diverted the attention to the black-and-tan dog lying on the veranda. 'This is one of Chime's latest litter. We've kept two of them and called them Bow and Echo. This is Bow. He seems to think he's the security officer for the homestead.' She chuckled and bent to ruffle his ears.

'Zoe, would you like to come for a walk to see the dogs and horses with me?' Claire asked. 'I shifted a mob of cattle this morning and haven't let the horses out of the yard yet.'

Hesitating for a moment, Zoe turned to Lola as though seeking approval.

Lola nodded and smiled encouragingly. ''Way you go. We'll be here when you get back.'

Zoe shot her grandmother a weak grin and followed Claire down the steps.

Lola breathed a quiet sigh of relief. *Let's pray Zoe's transition to life in the country is easier than she expected.*

*Z*oe trod carefully around the patches of dirt and manure, wishing she had worn her old sneakers instead of the new, white Nikes her father had bought her the week before. They were the only brand-name items she had ever owned, and the last thing she wanted was to ruin them.

Claire looked down at Zoe's feet—no doubt noticing her grass-hopping gait. 'Sorry, Zoe. I should have loaned you a pair of boots.'

Zoe squirmed, her face flushing with heat. 'It's okay. I'll be careful.'

Claire grasped her arm and swung her away from the kennels in front of them, steering her along a gravelled track. 'We'll come back to the dogs soon. You can change into a pair of gumboots at the stables.'

Relief and gratitude flowed through Zoe, despite

the suggestion of gumboots. A dim memory of a pair of bright-yellow wellies, just like Paddington Bear's, flashed through her, and her lips twitched. *I was about three when I wore them.*

Minutes later—sensibly kitted out in a battered pair of oversized, black-rubber boots—Zoe followed Claire to the round yard where five horses stood dozing.

'Hello, boys and girls. You've got a new visitor today.' Claire spoke to the horses as though they were family before turning to Zoe and pointing to each one as she introduced them. 'The big one with the spots on his rump is Splash. Those two are called Rusty and Flash.' She indicated the two smallest horses, their chestnut coats faded and shaggy. 'They were mine and Briony's ponies when we were young—both old and stiff now. But they still enjoy eating and are healthy, so they'll live out their lives here.'

Zoe leaped back as one of them approached and snorted, spraying droplets of snot over them.

'That's not very good manners, Rusty. Sorry about that, Zoe. Horses don't really care about personal hygiene.'

Zoe emitted a nervous giggle, her eyes glued to the two remaining horses, who seemed more interested in each other than the humans, standing nose to tail while they scratched each other's rumps with long, cream-coloured teeth.

'What about those two?' she asked.

'The bigger one is Akela. She's well-bred, and both Briony and I used to compete on her.'

'Compete?' Zoe frowned.

'Shows, dressage, jumping, pony club. Stuff like that.'

'Oh!' Except for the Brisbane Exhibition, commonly referred to as "The Ekka", Zoe had never been to a horse event.

Claire continued, 'The smaller, brown mare is called Tango. An old friend gave her to me as a wedding present a few weeks ago. She belonged to their daughter, who lost interest when she turned fourteen and human males became more important than her horse. Bobby didn't want Tango going anywhere she wasn't happy, so ... a win for me.'

'Wow. That's a pretty enormous gift.'

'Yeah. That's the thing about horse people, though. While some see them as money on four legs and treat them as such, others become so invested in the animal's happiness, finances don't count.'

'So, do you ride them all?'

Claire grinned at Zoe's wide-eyed question.

'Mostly. When we're busy with stock work, Mum rides Akela and I usually ride Splash. I've given Tango a few rides though, to ensure she's quiet and suitable for me to use for my students.'

'Students?' The whole horse thing was beyond anything Zoe had experienced.

'Since Rhys and I got married, I've become a bit more involved in the community—I lived in Sydney for a while and was at university before that. Anyway, good friends of Mum and Kirk's have their grand-daughter living with them now as her parents have recently separated and things are messy.' Claire paused and studied Zoe for a moment. 'Actually, Penny would be around your age, I think. Next time she comes for a lesson, you might like to come too and meet her?'

'Yeah. That'd be okay. I don't know anyone around here yet—except my grandparents and now you.'

'Great. It's a date. If you give me your phone number before you leave today, I'll text you when she's coming and nip down and pick you up from the store.'

'Really? You'd do that?'

Claire blinked at her. 'Of course, this is the country. We're a pretty friendly lot, you know.'

A chuckle escaped from Zoe, and Claire joined in as Tango reached over the rail and bumped her chin on her shoulder.

'Tango. Meet Zoe. She might be your next rider.' Claire winked at Zoe and rubbed the horse's nose.

A wave of terror mixed with elation gripped Zoe. The horses were huge and although part of her wanted to run away, the other part filled with exhilaration. If she learned to ride a horse, she would have one up on Amy and Natalia—and that would be a first.

'What does Rhys do ... and who's Kirk?'

'Rhys is the local cop. Since we married, we've been living in the quarters behind the police station. But because I have an office set up here—I'm a graphic designer—and I also help Mum with the farm work, I spend my days here.'

She paused, and Zoe took in her pretty, tanned face and kind eyes, her respect for this pleasant woman growing by the minute.

'And Kirk. He's Mum's partner. Came to Feather-wood Falls a couple of years ago and, long story short, he and my mother fell in love, so he stayed. Actually, he bought a little farm down the road and renovated the cottage—but now that I'm in town with Rhys, he lives here full time with Mum and is thinking of renting his house out.'

Zoe's head buzzed with all the information as Claire climbed the yard rails, strode across to the other side, and opened the gate wide. The horses raced out —Akela bucking and frisking while Tango and Splash trotted past, taking a wide berth to avoid her heels. The two old ponies shuffled at a hurried walk before stopping and putting their heads down to graze the second their tails cleared the closing gate behind them.

'Right. They'll be happy now. Let's meet the dogs.'

Zoe looked down. 'The boots?'

'Leave them on. You might as well wear them back to the house and keep your sneakers clean.'

Zoe tucked the Nike's under her arm and lengthened her stride to draw level with Claire.

A deafening racket of barking greeted them. Zoe ducked, putting a hand to her ear as Claire emitted a loud whistle.

The dogs silenced immediately.

'Sorry, Zoe. There's nothing wrong with their hearing and they are great at letting us know when someone's around that's not family. Trouble is, they only have one volume.'

Zoe met Claire's rueful grin with a smile. 'I suppose that's not a problem out here. Might start a neighbourhood row in the city, though.'

'Absolutely. Don't be worried. These dogs are all working kelpies and are well behaved. They won't jump up on you and if they want you to pat them, they will either sit or drop onto their bellies in front of you, inviting you to say hello.'

Zoe raised her eyebrows, not quite believing such behaviour could be true of these athletic-looking animals.

As Claire walked along the front of the wire enclosures, flinging each gate open as she went, the dogs emerged, ignoring the girls while they sniffed around and found a suitable spot to toilet. Then, one by one, they approached Claire and Zoe before watching

Claire's subtle hand signals and dropping onto their bellies in a row.

Zoe's jaw dropped. She had never seen such obedience—or devotion. The assortment of black and tan, and rich auburn animals seemed to smile, their tails wagging and their eyes glued to Claire's.

With Claire's encouragement, Zoe walked along the six dogs, reaching down, and allowing each to sniff her hand before touching them gently on the head.

The smallest red dog crawled toward her, tongue lolling as she attempted to lick Zoe's boot.

'This one is Bow's sister Echo. She's still got a lot to learn but is doing really well.'

'What are the others called?'

Pointing to each, Claire said, 'Meet Chime—she's the mum of the pups. Then this is Banjo, Drum, Flute, and Harp.'

'They're lovely. I saw a dog the same size as Echo the other day when I went for a walk around the village. It was with a nice lady who spoke to me.'

'Auburn hair or blonde?'

'The lady was blonde, and the dog was auburn.' Zoe giggled and Claire joined in.

'That would be Emma. She has Piccolo, another of this litter, and Ashleigh, one of the schoolteachers, has a black-and-tan pup she calls Jazz.'

'They all have music-associated names,' Zoe said.

'Yes. Mum and Dad have bred kelpies for years and,

being big music lovers, they gave all the dogs in the Featherwood Station bloodline names with a musical connection.'

'That's a cool idea,' Zoe breathed. 'I love music.'

'Do you? You and Emma would get along well then. She plays the piano and teaches music at the school, and she's got a beautiful voice. I remember hearing her sing at a Christmas concert one year when I came home from university. We all went to support the school and ended up having a great night. They're having the Christmas concert next week, I think—or the week after.' Claire paused for a moment, as though attempting to recall the date. 'Anyway, you'll be here, so we could all go again this year. It'll give you a chance to meet a few more locals.'

'Really?'

'Come on. Let's get back to the house for one of those lamingtons your clever grandmother has made. We'll leave the dogs out for a while to stretch their legs.'

As Zoe walked beside Claire, the kind woman who had been playing the piano sprang to mind. If she was the same Emma Claire had referred to, Zoe might walk that way again and listen. She would be quiet and hide behind a shrub. No one would even know she was there.

10

*E*mma lifted her head from the piano keyboard and frowned. It was her habit after returning home from school to let Piccolo out of her pen and spend fifteen minutes with her before sitting at the piano and allowing her favourite pieces to clear her head and settle her emotions. Once her musical interlude concluded, she and Piccolo would go for a long walk before dark.

'That girl is here again,' Emma whispered to Piccolo.

The pup's massive ears pricked up, and she turned her head to the side.

'I'm going to speak to her.'

Quickly and quietly, Emma slipped out the back door, leaving Piccolo inside, and hurried along the hedge-lined fence before rounding the shrub closest to the road. The same girl she had encountered on Sunday evening sat on the grass, her arms wrapped around bent legs and her forehead resting on her knees.

'Hello again.'

The girl leapt to her feet with wide eyes. Her pale face coloured to a deep pink, and she stuttered, 'S-sorry. I didn't mean to be nosey.'

Emma rested a hand on the girl's arm. 'Don't go.'

Poised to flee, the girl hesitated for an awkwardly long moment. Then her shoulders sagged, and she looked down, seemingly studying her sneakers.

Emma waited, willing the teenager to look at her.

She did.

'Don't feel bad. I'm humbled that you listen to me playing,' Emma said.

They stared at each other before Emma continued.

'My name's Emma. Would you like to come inside and join me at the piano?'

Zoe's cheeks returned to their usual pallor—her turquoise eyes the colour of the sparkling sea around the Whitsunday's coast where Emma had briefly holidayed with her mother a decade ago.

'Can I?' Incredulity illuminated Zoe's face.

'Of course. Come this way.'

Emma led her up the veranda stairs and through the French doors. Piccolo greeted them both like long-lost friends, and it took a few pats from Zoe and stern words from Emma before she lay down again. Then, after bringing a dining chair over to the piano, Emma placed it next to her stool and sat down.

'What would you like me to play? Sorry, I don't know your name.'

'It's Zoe.'

'Nice to meet you properly, Zoe. So ... visitor's choice?'

'I-I heard you playing "The Climb" on Sunday afternoon. I love that. Would you play it again for me ... please?'

'Of course.'

Without another word, Emma began. After the introductory notes, she cleared her throat and sang. Zoe joined in and Emma smiled at her encouragingly. They reached the chorus and increased their volume.

When the song ended, Emma placed her hands in her lap and turned to face Zoe. 'You have a beautiful voice, Zoe.' She rubbed a hand over her arm. 'Look, you've brought goosebumps to my skin.'

They both laughed. Emma's head spun with delighted surprise. *Please don't run off.*

'What shall we sing next?' Emma asked.

Zoe made no move to leave, and Emma's hopes rose. She wanted to hear more, both from and about this girl. Who was she? She certainly hadn't been a student at Featherwood Falls primary school, and she didn't recall having seen her in the queue of high-school students lined up at the bus stop.

'Can you play Nashville Cast's "Believing"? I used to sing it as a duet with the guy who took choir when I was in Brisbane.'

'I can try. I don't have the music for it but have heard it played enough times. I should be able to pick it up if you will sing it for me?'

As Zoe began, Emma closed her eyes and softly played—at first just the treble, and then, feeling the accompanying bass chords, she hummed along with her.

During the following half hour, they moved on to mutual favourites after the surprising revelation that Zoe had grown up listening to Leonard Cohen's "Hallelujah", songs by the Bee Gees, ABBA, and Eagles. They finally finished with "O Holy Night". It was Emma's favourite Christmas carol, and she told Zoe they weren't able to include it in the school concert as it was too difficult for the young children to sing.

Piccolo nudged Emma's elbow and placed a paw on her knee.

Emma laughed. 'I think Piccolo has had enough. We usually go walking at this time of day.'

Zoe jumped to her feet and stepped toward the door. 'Sorry. It's been really lovely singing again. Thank you.'

Emma stood and put out her hand. 'Don't feel you

have to rush off, Zoe.' She paused. Valuing her own privacy, she was reluctant to intrude but felt a deep need to know more about this girl. 'You're welcome to come again. I've really enjoyed our time together.'

'I'd love to ... if that's okay.'

'Perfect. Perhaps confirm it with your parents?'

'It'll be fine. I'm staying with ... family, and I'm sure they'll be cool about it. They're pretty busy anyway so won't miss me.'

Before Emma could address the girl's momentary hesitation, Zoe was leaping down the veranda steps. She paused at the bottom and turned to give Emma a shy wave before jogging along the road, exactly as she had only days earlier.

Emma shook her head and looked into the doggy eyes pleading with her—the pup's little body writhing with anticipation as her tail slapped against the floor. 'Okay, Piccolo. Let's go for a walk.'

Following the same route that Zoe had taken minutes earlier, Emma barely noticed where the dog led her. Her head was whirling and her skin tingled as the songs she and Zoe had sung replayed inside her head.

She was no expert, but what she had experienced over the past hour thrilled her to her core.

Whoever that girl is, her voice is beautiful.

11

*W*ith steps as light as smoke curling from a well-fed fire, Zoe pranced along the roadside. The usual fear that hung deep inside her was all but gone and she was unable to keep the smile from her lips. Her heart sang in time with the songs she hummed and, for the first time since her mother's death, she lifted her face to the late afternoon sun, relishing the caress of its warmth.

Stopping to pat Wattle as she passed by the kangaroo enclosure, she took time to study the animals. Most were grazing or hanging around the feed bins, clearly waiting for their late-afternoon meal, and Zoe noted their shiny coats and bright, intelligent eyes. Her respect for the time and effort her grandmother had put in lifted another notch.

You are quite amazing, Lola, Grandma, Nanna? What am I supposed to call you?

She continued to the back porch, removed her shoes, and pushed the door open.

A fragrant wave of spicy scents greeted her, the hint of cinnamon and nutmeg mingling with an overwhelming sense of optimism.

'Is that you, Zoe?' Lola's cheery call reached her from the shop kitchen.

'Yes. I'm back,' she replied as she followed the smell. Zoe smiled at her grandmother—the now familiar grey strands of hair that refused to be tamed standing like a halo around the older lady's flushed face and catching in the edges of her pink-framed glasses. 'Something smells nice.'

'I've got cinnamon scrolls in the oven—thought I'd pop some in the freezer, ready for the Christmas concert and get-togethers that seem to happen with a rush every December.' She waved a hand toward the heavy iron pot on the stove. 'And that's a chicken curry for dinner. Thought it'd be easier to keep an eye on it out here while I'm doing the scrolls.' Her smile met Zoe's. 'Did you enjoy your walk?'

Zoe nodded. 'Yes, thanks. I'm getting to know my way around now ... and I met a nice lady, so we talked for a while.'

'Oh? Who was that?'

'Yeah. Emma. Didn't get her last name, but she's

about Mum's age and has a lovely kelpie called Piccolo.' She hesitated as a flash of concern shone in Lola's eyes, fading as quickly as it had arrived. Her stomach flipped. Had she done something wrong? Was Emma an outsider in the town or someone the family had fallen out with? She couldn't imagine anyone not liking Emma—but then how would she know?

'That's lovely. Emma's a delightful woman—and well respected. She's been the teacher's aide at our little school for years. Grew up here.'

Relief flowed through Zoe. She had been about to tell Lola about the music but bit her lip instead. She would find out more before she divulged further information.

'Umm. I don't know what to call you,' Zoe said quietly.

Lola stepped closer and rested her hand lightly on Zoe's shoulder. 'Zoe, you can call me whatever you want to. I've always been called Lola, Mrs Brown, or Mum.' She grinned ruefully. 'You're my only grandchild, so you decide.'

'Well, I've never had a grandmother either—only Mrs Worth ...'

'Tell me about Mrs Worth,' Lola prompted gently.

'She was our neighbour, and I spent a lot of time with her, especially when Mum was sick. But we never knew much about her. I wasn't trying to be nosey, but sometimes if I asked her about her life, she would get

all tetchy and tell me it was time for me to go home—
even when Mum wasn't there. The only thing I found
out was that she had been married a long time ago but
had no children. She told me she had been a teacher,
which was pretty awesome because she knew a lot
about education and was really helpful with my
homework.'

'Have you phoned her or sent her a message since
you've been here?'

'Yeah. I texted her on Sunday night. I promised her
I would let her know where I was and that I was okay.'

'That's nice. I'm sorry I didn't meet her. It was
incredibly good of her to care for you ... after your
mum passed.'

Zoe shrugged. 'So, can I call you Nan? Grandma
sounds really old—and you're not really, are you?'

Lola laughed—a hearty, jovial explosion that
brought another smile to Zoe's face.

'That's sweet of you to ask. I don't think I'm old, but
I admit it's been a long time since I was sixteen. I'm
seventy-three and incredibly lucky I've had a happy
and healthy life.' Her face softened as she continued.
'And now I feel very blessed and delighted to have you
in our lives.' Lola inhaled sharply and kneaded her left
shoulder, seemingly unaware she was doing it.

'Hello, you two.'

Zoe whipped around, grateful for the distraction
while absorbing Lola's comment.

'Hi, Ryan,' she said, a new warmth colouring her cheeks. Despite accepting he was her father, he had said nothing about calling him "Dad", and she was grateful for that. Although referring to Lola as "Nan" was also a big step—probably for Lola as well–getting used to the idea that Ryan was her dad was taking time.

Ryan had spent the previous couple of days working with Frank—sorting and delivering mail and then helping repair fences and catching up on maintenance around the smallholding.

While Zoe was enjoying spending time getting to know her father and grandparents, she appreciated their unspoken understanding when waves of grief engulfed her at unexpected moments. On these occasions, she retreated to her room—sometimes not emerging to shower until everyone had gone to bed—and she felt secure in the peaceful silence that encompassed the home.

Guilt filtered its way through her. If circumstances had been different and her mother had survived, Catherine would have hounded her, wrapping her arms around her at every opportunity and encouraging her to "let it all out" and "talk to me". Catherine had been academic, vivacious, and popular, but common sense and quiet understanding hadn't been in her make-up. Instead, it had been Zoe who, from an early age, had checked the oven was turned off, the rubbish bin had been put out, and the doors were locked before they went to bed.

'Hey, I've had a call from work,' Ryan said, interrupting Zoe's train of thought.

Both Lola and Zoe looked at him—it was hard to miss the disappointment in his tone.

'And?' Lola prompted.

'They want me to return a couple of days earlier than my roster dictates. Three of the blokes in my section are off sick, leaving only me and one other guy able to finish this job.'

Zoe blinked, wondering what this meant for her.

'I'm sorry to have to leave you here so soon, Zoe. Will you be okay with that?'

She glanced at Lola, her eyebrows raised in question. 'I guess so. If it's okay?'

Lola smiled and flicked a dismissive hand at her son. 'Of course, it'll be fine. Have you told Zoe your plans yet?'

'No, sorry, Zoe. I was going to discuss it with you last night, but ... well, you went to bed early and I didn't want to interfere,' he trailed off lamely.

Zoe said nothing, jumping when the shop bell sounded behind them.

'I'll get that,' Lola said. 'You and Zoe have a talk in the lounge.'

～

ZOE PERCHED on the edge of the couch, facing Ryan as he leaned forward opposite her, his hands clasped loosely together and hanging between his knees.

'I know it's early days, Zoe, and you haven't had time to get to know your grandparents yet.'

Zoe sensed the "But" coming before he continued.

'Life has changed for us both—and now it's time to make plans that will suit us all and, hopefully, keep us happy.'

They stared at each other in silence for what seemed to be ages before he continued.

'I've given my notice at work.'

Straightening, Zoe's mind raced. Did that mean they were moving back to Brisbane?

'As you can see, my parents—your grandparents—are aging.'

She quirked an eyebrow. *Duh. You have been away a long time—or can't you count*? Squirming, she reminded herself Ryan was a nice guy. She liked him, especially as he treated her like an adult and not a child.

'Although they're both still fit and well,' Ryan continued, 'the past three days here have shown me how much help they need, even though they won't ask for it. So, if it's okay with you, I thought we'd stay for the summer holidays, see how you feel in the new year, and have a look at some schools that might suit you. I can help Mum and Dad out and perhaps put things in place to give them more time away from the business. What do you think?'

'I guess that's okay.' She shrugged. What were her choices? She couldn't live with Mrs Worth, and neither of her best friends had offered for her to even stay overnight with them. Not that she'd expected it. Amy's mum and dad worked long hours in their gardening business and, when at home, seemed to be constantly fighting. Her two younger brothers demanded all the energy her parents had to spare. The family consumed enormous quantities of takeaway food, and Amy accepted as many shifts as possible at her part-time coffee-shop job in order to get away from the chaos. Natalia was the opposite. Her well-meaning parents watched her every move, hovering over her studies, hobbies, and friends. They stifled and monitored all hints of independence and restricted the freedom Zoe appreciated.

Her attention returned to her father as he spoke again.

'I thought we might have a tour around the area tomorrow afternoon. Take a picnic and get Janet to come and mind the shop. I'd like to show you more than what's here in Featherwood Falls, so you can get a feel for the place.'

She nodded. 'Sure. That sounds okay.'

The discussion of Ryan's two-week absence reminded her of the invitations she had received. She could spend an hour each afternoon with Emma. Lola seemed happy for her to go for an afternoon walk, and if she received the riding lessons Claire had offered her and helped feed the native animals each morning, the time hanging around the shop would be minimised.

The more she thought about it, the more she wanted to do something she loved—and something completely different. Singing with Emma and learning to ride filled both criteria.

*T*heir three-hour drive had taken them on a wide circle around the local hotspots— popular walking tracks with lookouts over the valley and east toward Brisbane, and a lake dotted with dingy-filled anglers and children splashing and squealing as they played around the edges. After enjoying Lola's cinnamon scrolls washed down with a cup of tea, they visited a cheese-making factory and enjoyed sampling the wide array of tiny blocks varying in colour from white, blue-veined creams to a rich orange.

Anxious hope filled Lola's chest. Whenever Zoe's phone pinged as they drove through an area with a brief few moments of connectivity, it was as though no one else existed. Zoe's head would bend over the device as her fingers flew at lightning speed, tapping

out messages and sending them before the opportunity was lost. Once the reception died again, she'd stare
at her surroundings and appear to listen to Frank's
stories of various residents and incidents he had
encountered over thirty-plus years of delivering mail.
Lola sat quietly, the joey in her lap, watching Zoe,
worrying about her granddaughter's future, her health,
and her happiness. It had been less than a week since
they had met, and Lola was in awe of this pretty, heart-
broken sixteen-year-old. Her own flesh and blood.

It was late afternoon when Ryan pulled up beside
the store, waited for his passengers to climb out of the
car, and then drove around the back to park the vehicle
in the newly cleared-out garage.

Zoe carried the joey into the house while Lola
lugged the wicker basket containing the picnic
remnants through the adjoining door to the shop.
Frank remained outside, talking to an old man in a
battered hat who had pulled up to fuel his vehicle.

The woman behind the counter rushed forward,
reaching to take the basket from Lola.

'It's all right, Janet. I can manage.' Lola flapped her
hand, dismissing the woman's attention a little crossly.
She understood Ryan's encouragement for her and
Frank to slow down and accept help, but after four
decades of owning and operating the Featherwood
Falls Store and Post Office, she wrestled with a reluctance, a possessiveness that roiled inside her. In her

struggle to release the reins, her tone was sharper than she intended. 'How did you get on?'

'Great. It wasn't busy, and I'm used to operating the EFTPOS now—and the coffee machine,' Janet said.

'Good. Right, well, I'll empty this basket and let you head home.'

Janet met Lola's dismissal with wide, surprised eyes. 'No hurry, Lola. I can stay until closing time if you like. Mum's living with us now and she'll have the kids sorted and dinner on the table, so I don't need to worry.' She reached out and laid her hand on Lola's arm. 'And neither do you.'

Lola blinked back threatening tears. She didn't need Janet's compassion. *What's wrong with me? I'm grateful for the help. Only ...* Her shoulders sagged. Aging was like being on a roller-coaster. One minute you were fit, healthy, and on top of the world. The next ... exhaustion, niggling aches, and decades of memories reminding you that you have now reached the age bracket referred to as "elderly". A shortness of breath and the periodic pain in her left shoulder had become her latest annoyance.

She grunted a reluctant, 'Thank you,' and bent over the basket, removed the cloth-wrapped, leftover scrolls, and handed them to Janet. 'Here. Take these home for the family. We've had our fill today and they're best when fresh.'

'Thank you, Lola. The kids will love them. Why

don't you put your feet up for a while? It's quiet now and I can manage.'

Loath to leave her assistant, Lola bristled at the suggestion she might need a rest despite the breathlessness that caught her out once again. 'I won't be doing that, but if you're sure you're alright here on your own, I'll get dinner started and feed the animals.' Then, without waiting for Janet to reply, she swept out of the shop via the adjoining door and closed it firmly behind her.

'Are you alright?'

Lola softened at the sight of Zoe's concerned, pale face. 'Of course, love. I was thinking about what I can cook for dinner. Any suggestions?'

Zoe grinned. 'After those lovely cinnamon scrolls, I'm not very hungry. But if you'd like some help, I'm rather good at making lasagne.'

'Really?' Lola released the word without thinking. Zoe seemed so young and vulnerable. And yet her life —or at least the last few years—had clearly demanded more independence and responsibility than most of her age. 'Sorry, Zoe. I shouldn't be surprised. You're amazing.'

At the compliment, Zoe stood tall and beamed. Lola's heart squeezed.

'Alright. Let's make it together. You can give me your best tips and I'll give you mine,' Lola said.

While Zoe stirred the rich, meaty sauce, Lola assembled the rest of the ingredients, biting back the dozen questions she wanted to ask. It was too early. She hoped that with time, Zoe would share her memories, both good and bad, giving Lola a better understanding of the girl's past. For now, she had to be grateful she hadn't shown resentment or dissatisfaction over her move to Featherwood Falls. In fact, she had displayed little emotion. *One day, that will come— and I need to be ready.*

'You mentioned meeting Emma the other day.'

Zoe looked up. 'Yeah. I heard her playing the piano, so I stopped to listen.'

'Oh?' Lola nearly dropped the cheese she was grating. 'Do you like music?'

'Yeah. I used to sing in the school choir in Brisbane,' she replied, a wistful tone in her voice.

There'd been a number of times she had said something to Zoe, only for her to ignore her. It had taken Lola almost two days to discover the girl wasn't being rude, she simply hadn't heard Lola speak. The plugs blocking Zoe's ears were apparently conduits for listening to the music on her phone—which was almost always sticking out of her back jeans pocket. 'Do you play the piano?'

Zoe shook her head. 'No. I'd like to learn though. It was nice listening to Emma.'

Did Emma know who Zoe was? That she was Ryan's daughter? Something in Zoe's manner suggested not. Most people believed secrets were difficult to hide in a small community, but Emma was different. Despite the help she'd given to both Emma and her mother years earlier, neither woman had confided in Lola—or any of the other ladies who had stepped in—as far as she knew. A deep ache formed in the pit of Lola's stomach for Emma as she smiled at Zoe.

'Perhaps we could see if Emma would teach you? She's exceptionally good with the kids at school and runs the Christmas concert each year. Which reminds me ...' She stepped toward the calendar, adjusting her spectacles as she squinted at the small print in the squares. 'It's less than two weeks till the concert. We always attend—support the community. Ryan's swing won't be finished in time for him to come, but you'll be able to join us,' she finished happily.

'Would she? Teach me to play the piano, I mean?' Zoe's thoughts were clearly fixed on learning to play rather than the concert.

'I don't see why not. You'll have to ask her yourself. Don't worry about the cost. We're all here for you now and if that's something you'd like to do, then you will be given every opportunity.'

Illustrated hope lit the girl's usually neutral face.

Guilt at her earlier shortness with Janet stabbed at Lola. She swallowed, forcing all remnants of discontent from her thoughts. This was what she should focus on now. Not the shop. Not the post office. Ryan was right —no matter how hard it would be. It was time to take a step back and get to know this beautiful young woman —her granddaughter.

She met Zoe's astounded grin with a smile as a leap of confidence cradled her heart.

13

Zoe scurried along the track, her fingers crossed, hoping Emma hadn't been held up at school. The late-afternoon sunshine still held enough heat to make her wish she had grabbed a cap to shade her eyes, while a gentle breeze lifted the hair from her shoulders and blew it across her face. Tucking the strands behind her ears, she swung her gaze from the path to the hills bathed in shades of purple and grey, and to the vivid blue sky above.

It was quite beautiful. Not like the sky in the city, but bigger and yet somehow more inviting. A jet plane soared high in the distance, the faint engine roar reaching her long after it at passed overhead. She recalled the conversation with her father about having to fly off to central Queensland for his last shift.

He seemed genuinely disappointed he wouldn't be around for two weeks and had given her a brief, awkward hug before he left, as though it was as unfamiliar for him as it was for Zoe. It had felt nice. He smelled of soap and spicy aftershave, and she'd breathed in the freshly ironed cotton of his shirt as she pressed against his chest—while also cringing at the memory of the stiff rejection she had shown both Amy and Natalia's fathers when they attempted to give her a goodbye hug before she left Brisbane. Women, and mothers especially, she could handle. But no matter how hard she had tried, memories of Adrian's body odour and metallic, sour breath had clouded her senses over the last four years, turning her off getting close to any male. It had been hard not to gag whenever he came within two metres of her, and she'd wondered over and over how her mother put up with him.

Desperation, I suppose.

She would never forget the first time she arrived home to find Catherine sprawled naked over the bed, unable to be woken. Terrified she was dead, Zoe had run to Mrs Worth's and banged on her door. After checking Catherine's pulse, the older woman had called an ambulance and, while they waited, ordered Zoe to find a nightie. Together, they had wrestled it over her mother's leaden arms and head. As if that horror hadn't been enough, the shock of being told her mother was suffering from a drug overdose had been much, much worse.

As the recurrences increased, Zoe had learned to control her emotions. Her panicked fear had turned to resignation. There had been nothing she could do except express how much she loved and needed her mother. The first twelve years of her life had been a bonus—a blissful dream. After that, Catherine's choices had ruled their lives and broken Zoe's heart.

HER STEPS GREW hesitant as she knocked on Emma's door.

'Coming.' Emma's voice called from the depths of the cottage seconds before a sharp bark reverberated through the air.

The door flew open, and Emma stood there, her cheeks flushed and her usually neat, bobbed hair dishevelled. 'Hi, Zoe. Come in.' She grinned and looked down at Piccolo. 'We were having a wrestle with the tea towel.' She stepped back and held up a torn cloth, rolling her eyes. 'Someone dragged it out of the laundry basket while I was getting changed.'

Zoe grinned. 'Naughty Piccolo.'

'Would you like a drink? I'm about to make myself a cup of tea.'

'Thanks. I'll have a glass of water, please?'

'Sure.' Emma filled the kettle, reached for a glass from the overhead cupboard, and passed Zoe a chilled bottle from the fridge. 'Help yourself.'

Zoe cleared her throat, her heart pounding. 'I-I was wondering if you would teach me how to play the piano?' There—it was out. She held her breath and met Emma's surprised expression.

'I'm not a piano teacher, Zoe. I had two years of lessons when I was young and have taught myself since then. I'm not sure I'm qualified?' Emma spoke slowly, her tone questioning.

'But you play so well. Couldn't you teach me something?'

Emma lowered her shoulders as their eyes met. 'Are you sure about this?'

Zoe's heart sank, and she shrugged. 'It's okay if you don't want to. Maybe we could just get together to sing sometimes.'

Emma reached for Zoe's hands and gripped them tightly. 'Zoe, I would be delighted to teach you what I know, but you would need to do a lot of practice. Have you got a piano at home?'

Zoe shook her head. 'I didn't think of that.' She choked back the lump in her throat. 'Forget I asked.'

The kettle switched off, and Emma turned to pour the hot water over a teabag.

As she watched, Zoe barely moved, merely taking slow breaths and cursing silently. What had she been thinking? She must be mad to have even considered it. In the city, playing an instrument hadn't crossed her mind ... But here, amongst the green hills and peaceful, friendly people, she had let her stupid heart rule her head.

She turned and hurried to the door.

'Zoe. Don't go!' Emma grabbed her arm. 'Please. I understand how you feel, but we need to talk about how it could work for us both. Come and sit down.'

She released Zoe's arm, picked up her tea, and pulled out two kitchen chairs from their positions under the table. 'I'm at school from eight in the morning until four. You know now that most days I play for an hour before taking Piccolo for a walk. What about ...?' She stared at Zoe. 'There's less than two weeks of school left. Then we have until the end of January before we begin again. How about we spend what time we've both got to sing together until the end of term, then, when I'm home all day in the holidays—and if you're not doing anything—we could begin some simple lessons? While I'm outside gardening, you could continue practicing here and we'll see how you get on. Perhaps you'd like to walk with Piccolo and me after our music sessions some evenings. That way we can go over things again and ... well, get to know one another better.' She sat back in her chair, her head tilted slightly in question.

Tears prickled Zoe's eyes. Emma was right. They

didn't know one another very well, and yet she was prepared to trust Zoe and give her a chance. 'Thank you,' she breathed with a quavering smile.

'I've just thought about something else.' Emma chewed her lip. 'How would you feel about helping me at the Christmas concert—maybe supporting the children's singing while I play?'

'Could I do that, though? I mean, would that be okay with the principal?'

'I'm sure Quinn would be delighted. I'll have a chat with him and see what we can come up with.' She put her empty mug on the table. 'Now let's sing a few songs —brighten us both up.'

14

---

*E*mma waved goodbye to Zoe, frowning with concern at the long shadows forming in the garden and the sparrows squabbling in the thick foliage of the May bush. Estimating she still had thirty minutes of daylight, she shoved her feet into her joggers, clipped the lead onto Piccolo's collar, and headed up the track.

Meeting the junction, where the left-hand fork was clear and well-trodden as it led to the village shop, they took the less-used, right-hand path. Narrow and over-grown underfoot, it forced them to slow and Piccolo swung from side to side, her nose to the ground. It wasn't a track they'd frequented but it provided steep inclines to test their fitness and pretty flora with views to enhance their walk.

Emma knew exactly how far they could travel before turning for home prior to darkness falling and the trail becoming fraught with tripping hazards. For years, she and Ryan had ridden their horses or walked this way in single file, stopping frequently to steal a kiss. At the top, over an hour's walk from the town and snuggled into a hollow in the lee of the hill, stood a timber-cutter's hut. Its solid, rough-hewn walls and corrugated-iron roof had provided shelter for both animals and humans for decades—and for Emma and Ryan, it had been their secret place. In the early years of Maureen's illness, Emma had escaped here whenever she could. Then, two years after Ryan's departure, she had perched on a log facing the hut and cried like a baby, swearing she would not come this far again. Her visits had been futile. Ryan was not coming back and there was no point dwelling on the past. She would move on.

In the previous decade, she had made only one excursion to the hut. It had been following her mother's death and, with the pressure of caring for the woman and the secrets they'd both held, Emma had burned with a need to return to a place that had once offered complete privacy, love, hope, and a happy future. On that visit, a deep-seated sadness had paralysed her. Dirty, forlorn windows blanketed by cobwebs, the loose, flapping iron on a corner of the roof, and the moss-covered bench leaning precariously on the broken veranda floorboards had reminded her that nothing was as it should be.

Since Piccolo had joined her life, she couldn't resist varying the inquisitive little dog's walks, providing them both with fresh smells, intermittent, breathtaking views, and a sense of being alone with nature. So, she had weakened and begun to trek the old path once again.

Increasing her pace, she dwelt on Zoe's visit. While the girl appeared quiet and well-behaved—and sang beautifully—Emma knew little more about her now than she had the day they met. After forty-two years of life in the village, almost every resident was familiar to her, especially as most newcomers had at least one child attending the local school or were parents and grandparents of children she'd helped in the past. So where did Zoe fit in? Was she the older sister of one of the students? She'd mentioned staying with family. Perhaps that was the connection.

A ruckus in the tree above interrupted her thoughts as three white-headed pigeons took flight. In the absence of the evening sun that had shimmered on the leaves only minutes before, the bush had taken on a gloomy, unsettled atmosphere. She shivered.

'Come, Piccolo! Time we headed for home.'

The pup looked up from several metres away where she had been nosing a hole in the ground. Disobeying Emma's call, she attempted to scamper further before coming to a sudden halt as she reached the end of the extension rope Emma gripped firmly in her hand.

'You little monkey. Come!' Emma ordered.

For a second, Piccolo met Emma's stern stare before returning sheepishly and tangling herself in the leash.

Emma shortened the lead until Piccolo stood beside her with less than two metres of leeway.

'Lucky I didn't let you have a free rein tonight—isn't it, missy? If I had, I suspect you and I would've played cat and mouse until well after dark.'

As though understanding every word, Piccolo pressed against Emma's legs and willingly trotted down the hill toward home.

The words of the song "The Climb" played over in Emma's head, and she hummed the tune. She and Zoe had run through the Christmas carols scheduled for the concert, then had finished with what was clearly one of their mutual favourites. A thought sprang to Emma's mind, and she smiled to herself. What if, after the standard routine of school presentations, singing, and acting the children's version of the nativity scene or a musical play, this year they ended with a duet—she and Zoe? Last year, one of the fathers had recited a poem he'd written about school days to conclude the presentation. Another year, three ex-pupils who had formed their own band played a bracket of songs unrelated to Christmas. It didn't have to all be about the festive time of the year. Featherwood Falls had always seen the concert as an opportunity to get together and celebrate all things communal, including the enormous spread of multicultural food that weighed the trestle tables down afterwards.

Her heart gave a little skip as she planned the performance. It would be a wonderful way to introduce Zoe to the community. Featherwood Falls was a welcoming village, and it would give Zoe a chance to widen her circle of friends.

With the details churning in her mind, she charged along the wider part of the track, pushed the picket gate open, and took the front steps two at a time.

ola and Ginny sat in the shade of the massive avocado tree on the western side of Featherwood homestead, looking across the house paddock to the stables and round yard. From the top rail where she was positioned, Claire called encouragement to Zoe, who was mounted on Tango— the steady little brown mare Zoe had fallen in love with.

It had been eight days since Zoe's first riding lesson. Although Lola had not ridden since childhood, she had been a supporter and pseudo-grandmother to both Ginny's girls, leaving Frank to run the store one Sunday each month while she joined them at Pony Club. After witnessing their growth and increased confidence, she passionately believed having horses to care for, exercise, and spend their pocket-money on was what had helped shape Briony and Claire into kind, responsible adults.

Now it was happening again. Lola could only imagine how nervous Zoe must have been initially—especially when the other student Claire had expected did not turn up–Zoe had returned to the store bursting with vitality and a wide smile on her face. During Zoe's first week of lessons, Claire had collected her at seven-thirty each morning and delivered her home again before ten. It seemed Zoe had hoped for longer lessons, but as each day passed, colour brightened her cheeks, her eyes sparkled, and her energy increased.

'Do you want to come and see how I'm progressing?' Zoe had asked on day seven.

Lola had jumped at the invitation, ensuring Janet was installed in the shop at least half an hour before she and Zoe hopped in the car and whipped up to the farm, relieving Claire of the free daily return taxi service.

'Look!' Lola flapped a hand in Ginny's face and stood up. 'She's trotting now—and rising nicely. Hardly even a bump.'

Ginny linked arms with Lola and together they ambled toward the stables.

As they drew near, Claire glanced over her shoulder and held her hand up in a stop signal. They waited, and Lola held her breath as the pony changed into a smooth canter.

'That's good, Zoe. Keep those heels down and sit up straight!' Claire called.

Her mouth set in a firm line and her shoulders back, Zoe gripped the reins until her knuckles shone white.

After cantering three laps of the round yard, Claire called again, 'Steady now, Tango. Trot on.'

The pony reduced its pace to a slow trot before dropping into a walk.

Zoe lifted her gaze from the horse's ears to Lola and Ginny, who were now leaning on the railing beside Claire.

'That was lovely, dear,' Lola yelled, unable to keep the excitement from her voice.

Zoe beamed, puffing as they approached the other women, and halted. 'That was my first canter.' She grinned at Claire. 'You were right. It's more comfortable than trotting—just a bit scary when you first start.'

'Of course. A week ago, you were frightened to get on, remember? Look at how much confidence you've gained and how well you're doing.'

'The main thing is,' Lola added, 'are you enjoying it?'

Zoe nodded enthusiastically. 'It's awesome. And Tango is so sweet. She doesn't mind me making mistakes. Claire said in another week when Penny comes out here, we'll both be good enough to go out in the paddock riding with her.'

'Yeah. I just have to work out who's going to ride which horse,' Claire laughed. 'Tango is perfect for you both, but because Penny is taller than Zoe, she'd be better on Splash. Zoe can ride Tango and I'll ride Akela.'

'Who's Penny?' Lola asked.

'Val and Neil's granddaughter from over at Kallala.' Ginny's brow creased in a concerned frown.

'Of course,' Lola blustered. Wracking her brain, she vaguely recollected Ginny mentioning something about Val and Neil's son and wife going through a nasty divorce. Penny must be their daughter. She'd only met the girl once, soon after Val and Neil had moved to the district and when Penny and her parents had visited for a long weekend. They'd come to Featherwood Falls for a barbeque and Lola had not been impressed with the awkward, spoilt fourteen-year-old. Silently, she hoped the girl had improved. Penny was obviously the other student Zoe had expected to be having lessons with.

As though reading Lola's mind, Claire said, 'Penny's grown up a lot and I think she and Zoe will get along well. She's a bright girl but has never had much to do with animals, so I was surprised when she asked me to teach her to ride. She was staying with her grandparents during the September holidays. Lonely, I guess.'

No different to Zoe then. Except Penny had the luxury of a private-school education and wealthy parents—and her mother was still alive when Zoe's was not. Lola clamped her lips in a firm line, annoyed she had allowed herself to think that way. She had always strived to look at the bright side of everything and never let negativity invade her opinions.

What is happening to me? I'm becoming a crabby, old woman.

She drew a deep breath and focused on Zoe again, her chest swelling with pride as she watched her.

'That will be nice for them both,' Ginny said.

For a few seconds, Lola looked at her friend blankly. What was she was talking about? *Loneliness. That's right. If Penny is lonely, then perhaps Zoe is too?* She studied the enthusiastic expression on her granddaughter's face and gave a small shake of her head, allowing a smile to lift her lips and ignoring the niggling pain that ran across her left shoulder.

No. I think she's okay.

WITH THE HORSES UNSADDLED, groomed, and released into the paddock, the four of them returned to the house for a cup of tea and one of Ginny's freshly made scones, covered with lashings of strawberry jam and whipped cream.

Lola patted her stomach, her face alight with a satisfied grin. 'Thank you both once again, Ginny and Claire. Zoe and I had better get back to the shop or Janet will think we've deserted her.'

Zoe stood and gathered the empty mugs. 'Yeah, thanks heaps for this morning, Claire—and Mrs Shepherd. Those scones were delicious.'

Ginny waved a hand dismissively. 'Please call me Ginny, Zoe. Everyone else does.'

'Except for Uncle Donald,' Claire chipped in. Shooting Zoe a quick wink, she continued, 'He calls Mum, Virgin-ia.' She emphasised the first six letters, and Zoe raised her eyebrows.

Ginny rose to her feet, her mouth clamped and her eyes flashing with anger. 'That'll be enough about him.'

The air weighed heavily with tension. Lola gathered her cardigan from the chair back and began walking to the veranda. 'Thanks again, Ginny. We'll see you tomorrow, Claire?'

'Sure. Can we make the lesson a bit later—say ten o'clock? We've got hay down and Andrew's coming to bale it tomorrow night. I want to get it raked early in the morning before the sun gets too hot,' Claire said.

Zoe looked at Lola. 'Is that okay with you, Nan?'

It was the first time Zoe had used the endearment, and Lola grinned, delight bubbling inside her. 'Of course.'

'Are you doing anything tomorrow evening, Zoe?' Claire asked. 'You might like to come and join us. We could have a barbeque first, then you can ride in the truck with Mum. She manoeuvres the loader, scooping up the bales while Kirk and I stack the hay.'

Ginny added, 'Sounds like a great idea. Lola, why don't you and Frank come too?'

Lola glanced at Zoe, aware of her routine dog walk with Emma. 'Zoe? I'm sure Emma will understand if you send her a text.'

The girl nodded, her eyes alight. 'Love to.'

16

*A*s they cruised up the slope toward Featherwood Station the following evening, Lola shared with Zoe a synopsis of Andrew's life, as if to reassure her there would be no strangers to make her feel uncomfortable.

'He's just finished uni, so he's managing Glenrowan, the farm next door, at the moment for his father. Nothing like his dad though, thankfully—that's Donald, the black sheep of the family,' she chattered on. 'Don't know his mother, Sarah, very well. She rarely comes to family functions and has led a fairly separate life with her accountancy colleagues. But she and Andrew are close, even though Andrew spent most of his childhood holidays on Featherwood Station when Lyndon was alive—that's Claire's and Briony's father.'

Zoe said nothing, conjuring up pictures of a young smart-arse she would be expected to be polite to. Probably a snobby, privately educated "mummy's boy" or a ragged youth with his cap on backwards and nothing sensible to say.

Then she remembered Claire's mention of him baling the hay. Surely that involved operating some sort of fancy farm machine. If he could do that, and had been to uni, he couldn't be too stupid.

An hour later, and after being unprepared to meet someone so "normal", she pushed the pieces of steak around her plate with a fork, taking little notice of what she was eating, her attention focused on the young man leaning against the veranda rail.

He wasn't handsome in that dark, mysterious way of love stories, nor was he even particularly good looking. But since Claire's introduction of her cousin Andrew, Zoe found herself entranced. He'd offered a work-worn but clean, dry hand, squeezing hers gently when she tentatively offered it. His warm grin and thin, clean-shaven face surprised her in a good way. No spotty teenager with fluffy chin hair here, nor the unshaven look of those students who had matured early—in looks, if not in mentality.

'I'm sorry to hear about your mum, Zoe,' he'd said, his grey eyes filling with compassion.

She'd nodded silently, snapping her gaping mouth shut, awkward with her loss of words. The last thing she'd wanted was him thinking she was a gawping teenager.

As the evening progressed, Zoe's nervousness eased, absorbing the relaxed interactions between him and Claire. Both tall, thin, and sandy-haired, the family likeness was transparent. Andrew's smile encompassed them all, his grey eyes shining with happiness. His easy, almost gangly strides as he ferried platters of meat and salad from the kitchen to the veranda spoke of a teenager, while rippling arm muscles and the bond he seemed to have with Claire suggested a close, sibling-like maturity.

As he and Claire joked, Zoe envied their uncomplicated chatter. Her own circumstances had prevented her from experiencing such a connection, and it seemed as foreign to Zoe as her horse-riding lessons had been.

Zoe stared at him now, reflecting on how easy it was to mis-judge a person.

He looked away from Claire, meeting Zoe's gaze, and smiled. 'What sort of school year did you have, Zoe?'

She shrugged. 'Okay.'

'Any favourite subjects or activities?' he prompted.

Swallowing, she answered tentatively. 'Science, maths ... everything really.'

He raised his eyebrows. 'Great. They were my favourites, too. What about sport?'

'I like tennis.'

Elbowing Claire, Andrew grinned. 'As soon as we get that new fence around the courts, we'll have another player to join our merry band of tennis enthusiasts.'

He explained how the fortnightly get-together at the local courts was on hold for a few weeks as the community grant Claire had applied for had finally been approved, and now they were waiting for the materials to arrive so a working bee could be arranged and the new fencing erected around the venue. As he chatted, firing the occasional question at Zoe, she responded with shy, stilted words—his probing was not done intrusively like most adults, but more like a genuinely interested friend might be after being away for some time.

'I like music and singing too.'

'Awesome. I muck about on the guitar sometimes. Not very well, but enough to enjoy myself. Maybe one day we can get together for a jam.'

She grinned then, a sense of calm and inclusion washing over her, tinged with excitement.

He pointed to her plate. 'Better get that down you. Dessert's coming up, then we've got a paddock full of hay to bale.' He winked before turning his grin to Claire as she plonked a pile of dessert plates on the table. 'Feeling strong and energetic, Claire? Your mate over there looks weary tonight.'

Zoe followed his gaze to Kirk, the gigantic, bearded man they had introduced to her as Ginny's "other half" when she had first visited Featherwood Station. Zoe noted the deep creases across his forehead and either side of his mouth, suggesting he had the weight of the world on him as he scraped the barbeque plate clean and buffed it with paper towels.

'Nah,' Claire snorted. 'Kirk always looks like that, ay, Kirk!'

'What? You lot talking about me again.' He smiled at Zoe, a row of straight, white teeth highlighting his grey-streaked black beard.

She grinned back, recalling her first impressions of him. He had reminded her of Hagrid from the Harry Potter books she had poured over as a child, and she had taken an immediate liking to this quiet and gentle giant in much the same way she had with Ryan. Kirk had been at the stables constructing a new row of stalls to allow for Claire's growing band of horses, and it had been Kirk who had given her the confidence to sit on Tango that first day. Despite her desperation to hide any fear, she had frozen, unable to move. He had grasped her bent left leg by the shin and lifted her one-handed into the saddle as though she weighed no more than a two-year-old, murmuring encouragement and recalling his own early riding experiences. They had made her laugh, and she relaxed. Then, after watching for the first few minutes, reassuring her with every step, he'd returned to hammering and sawing throughout the lesson. His presence had given her the faith that she had it in hand—there was nothing to be afraid of and everything to enjoy.

'So, Zoe, when am I going to meet this father of yours?' Kirk asked.

Zoe blinked, jolted from her reverie. She had assumed everyone knew Ryan. 'He's working his last block of shifts at the moment and should be home sometime this weekend. He's somewhere that doesn't have great mobile reception, so I haven't had a text for a couple of days.'

'Okay. When he's back, we'll have to get together again then.'

The sudden flush of warmth wrapped around Zoe like a wool blanket. She smiled. The sense of loneliness that had prevailed for the past weeks, regardless of the attention everyone she'd met had offered, was fading fast. These kind people displayed a genuine desire to have both her and her father in their lives—and she liked that.

AN HOUR LATER, Zoe climbed into the truck cabin before lifting her knees to allow Chime to follow her and nestle at her feet.

'Doesn't she mind sitting on the floor with nothing to look at?'

Ginny shook her head, her brown, shoulder-length hair flicking over her face. Tucking it behind her ears with one hand, she reached down and patted the dog gently. 'No. She doesn't mind at all. Just wants to be near us—and she actually enjoys the rhythm of the engine while we putter around in circles.'

Zoe placed one foot on either side of the dog, bracing herself with a hand on the dashboard as the truck moved forward. She turned and peered through the back window as the hay loader, bolted to the side of the truck, clanked before whirring into action. Small prongs fixed to chains looped around the steep ramp grasped the first bale as the steel scoop shot it upward. Fascinated, Zoe's eyes fixed on the bale as it climbed to the small platform where Kirk snatched it up with two hand-held hooks, one on either side of the blue twine that held the compressed lucerne together. Then he swiftly plonked it at the front of the truck tray. Before he had it in position, the second bale appeared and Claire grabbed it, stacking it next to the first.

Stars appeared in the indigo sky and Zoe leaned out of the window to study them before the bright lights of the tractor and baler turned the corner and shone toward her. For the next few minutes, the vehicle and spotlights fused together, creating a world as bright as a sunny day. Ginny explained what was happening alternately with silent concentration as she steered the truck and loader to nudge each bale from the wavering row in front of them into the perfect alignment required by the loader.

A second layer of hay was quickly added to the first as they circumnavigated the paddock again and again, the bales on the ground reducing as their turns became tighter.

Zoe jerked forward as Ginny braked suddenly.

'Sorry, Zoe. I missed that bale and the next few are crooked. Do you think you could straighten them for me?'

Zoe looked at her blankly for a second before understanding the request. 'Sure.' She opened the door and jumped down, landing as lightly as a cat.

In the beam of the truck lights, she grabbed the two strands of tightly fastened baling twine and shuffled the first bale into the same alignment as those already picked up, huffing with surprise at the unexpected weight.

Then, jogging to the next one, she repeated the process.

The temperature had dropped, and Zoe was grateful for Ginny's insistence she wore a jacket. The air filled with the earthy scent of fresh, grassy lucerne and the hint of dew beginning to descend, and Zoe grinned with surprise at how much she was enjoying being in the middle of a hay paddock. While the vehicle lights were no match for the illuminated streets and blazing sirens of the city, the overhead vista of pearly stars and milky rivers traversing the blackness took her breath away. She bumped her knees against another bale and glanced over her shoulder. Ginny's silhouette moved, and it took a moment for Zoe to realise she was passing Claire and Kirk a drink of water from the bottle that had been sitting on the seat between them. She hauled the final wonky bale into place.

'Don't worry, guys. I've got this,' she whispered with a grin.

IT WAS after ten that night when Andrew pulled up at the rear of the store.

Zoe grabbed her bag and slid out of the ute. 'Thanks heaps for the lift.'

'No worries. We couldn't have Lola and Frank waiting until we'd finished, when that could have been anywhere between nine o'clock and midnight.' He grinned. 'If you're bored tomorrow, you can always get Frank to drop you off to help unload the truck,' he finished lightly.

She chuckled, already feeling the pull of her shoulder muscles from the little she had done. 'I reckon I'll leave that to you. Anyway, I promised Lola

I'd help in the shop tomorrow. She's teaching me to use the coffee machine.'

'Awesome! I'll give you a couple of days to master it, then I'll call in for a cappuccino.'

Zoe snorted a brief giggle and gave him a thumbs-up sign. 'See you then.'

'See ya.' He waved out the open window as he drove off.

Putting her key in the lock, she grinned to herself. It was nice to have a male friend who wasn't either making sexual innuendoes or ribbing her for being a "Miss Smarty-pants" when she topped the class. With the age difference between them, surely Andrew wasn't interested in any boyfriend-girlfriend stuff—and neither was she.

It was only as she crept quietly through the living room toward her bedroom that her stomach did a little flip as she realised two things. The first was that even when sitting in the car next to Andrew, her nostrils had not even tingled with the memory of that horrible metallic smell that was Adrian. The second was she hadn't sent or received a single text to or from either Amy or Natalia all day—her best friends.

17

*E*mma got up from the piano and opened the French doors. A sneaky, cool breeze had woken her early, and she had risen before the sun, hurrying along the road with Piccolo before thunderous clouds darkening the sky released their contents.

When it arrived, the rain lasted only minutes, beginning seconds after they returned from their walk and saturating her garden with a welcome drink. But by the time they had eaten breakfast, Emma was ready for school, and Piccolo was safely locked in her pen, the clouds had cleared. Now, at four-thirty in the afternoon, the air was damp and sticky, as though sending a warning it was too early to be complacent and hang the washing out just yet.

She smiled at Zoe, breathing a sigh as the breeze

fluttered the curtain and blew through the room. 'That's better.'

Zoe looked up for a second, then returned her gaze to her fingers, counting quietly to the tick of the metronome as both hands travelled up and down the keyboard, religiously practicing scales.

When she had completed each exercise Emma had set her, she stopped and pursed her mouth and turned to Emma. 'Am I doing it right?'

'Absolutely,' Emma said gently, resting a hand on Zoe's arm. 'But remember, we will not concentrate on scales or any simple pieces for you just yet. Let's get this concert over with first and then you can spend as much time as you like sitting here giving those fingers a workout.'

Zoe frowned, her earnest face strained with determination. 'Yeah. I know. I'm jumping the gun a bit. But I really want to learn.'

'And you will, Zoe. You have the drive, the intelligence—and the perfect, long fingers that will make playing easier for you than for me.' She held out her small hands, her fingers outstretched and the unvarnished nails neatly trimmed.

Their eyes met, and they both laughed.

'Okay. You win,' Zoe said. 'I suppose we've both got enough stuff to do before school finishes.'

'Sure have.' Emma glanced up at the clock on the kitchen wall before studying Zoe's sparkling turquoise eyes, delighted with the changes a bare three weeks in Featherwood Falls had made to this lovely girl. 'Are you and your Brisbane friends going to catch up over the Christmas holidays?'

Zoe shrugged. 'Doubt it. Amy's parents are too busy, and Amy's got a boyfriend. Now she's working full time at the café she doesn't text me much.'

Emma ached at Zoe's defeated tone. 'What about your other friend? Natalia, was it?'

'She messages. But she's finished school for the year, and her family is going to Japan for a skiing holiday. She said where they stay is quite remote so she might not text as often. Neither Amy nor Natalia have phoned me since I came here.' She shot Emma a rueful look, her head tilted. 'I read that as maybe neither of them are the friends I thought they were.'

Emma rested a hand on Zoe's arm reassuringly. 'I'm sure they don't see it that way. It's probably got more to do with your age and circumstances. You're all young women now, each going a different path to one you've trod the past few years. If they're faithful friends, you will keep that bond, even if you don't get together or talk as much as you used to.'

Emma cringed at her own advice, a brief stab of bitterness distracting her thoughts. So, what had happened to the friendship she and Ryan had believed would last forever?

Zoe nodded, her face brightening. 'Yeah. Maybe.'

Piccolo got off her bed and walked to Zoe, resting her head on her lap as though feeling the girl's uncertainty. Zoe stroked the dog's head gently and smiled at her.

Emma peered at the sky through the open doors. 'Come on. I reckon we're in for another shower soon. Let's run through our favourite songs one more time, then you'd better head for home—and I'll take Piccolo for her walk.'

Zoe swung around, pressing her palms together. 'Emma. Tomorrow, if it's not raining, can I come walking with you both again? We could spend less time here and more time walking. I think Piccolo would like that.'

They both laughed as Piccolo slapped her tail on the wooden floorboards.

'I think she's saying that's a great idea.' Emma sat beside Zoe and played the opening chords for "The Climb".

AFTER MORNING SHOWERS, a cool change breathed over the valley the following afternoon. Both Emma and Zoe wore jeans and a jumper as they sat at the piano, running through the list of songs to be performed the following evening.

Twitching with unbridled energy, Piccolo nudged

both of them every few minutes until they gave up and ended their music session early.

'Look at her. Anyone would think I haven't walked her for a week—not less than twelve hours ago.' Emma frowned at the dog.

'I saw you through my bedroom window,' Zoe said.

Emma shot her a curious glance and opened her mouth to ask where she lived before changing her mind. It wasn't important. 'I took her for a lap of the town because of the rain. It was short and apparently Piccolo doesn't think that counts in her daily routine.'

Zoe looked at Emma's kitchen clock. 'I'll come with you if you want to take her now. I've got heaps of time before I have to be home.'

'Great.' Emma stood and patted Piccolo before crossing the room and picking up her walking shoes. Shoving her feet into them, she pointed to Zoe's sneakers on the mat inside the back door. 'Does it matter if those get muddy?'

Zoe shook her head. 'No. They're my old ones—and I can scrub them.'

Within minutes, they were striding up the track, Piccolo hauling on the lead as though she was a police dog tracking a wanted criminal.

Taking the less-used path, Emma sucked in a breath and slowed to allow Zoe to catch up. 'Are you okay if we go this way? It looks like Piccolo is.'

Zoe grinned at her and nodded.

They chatted amicably as they walked, stopping intermittently to inspect emerging wildflowers and odd-shaped fungi clinging to the damp undergrowth. With the lead wrapped firmly around her wrist, Emma let Piccolo weave back and forth, the dog alert to anything that moved or emitted a smell, while they stepped around patches of gooey mud and hard-to-see roots that threatened to trip them. The sun shimmered on damp leaves, providing a soft, golden light as they passed and hinting it was not as late as the hands of Emma's watch showed.

'Hey, look!' Zoe pointed as the words exploded from her.

Emma followed the line of her arm, a sudden, possessive stab of nostalgia temporarily paralysing her. Zoe was pointing to the timber-cutter's hut. Her hut. Her and Ryan's.

'It's not far. Can we have a look?'

Emma clamped her lips together in a hard line. 'It's further than it appears, Zoe. By the time we reach it and then walk home again, it will be well after dark and your family might worry. Our mobile phones don't work up here, so you can't send them a message.'

Zoe met Emma's stern face with narrowed eyes. 'Is there something weird about it?' Zoe dropped her voice to a whisper. 'Like someone died there or was murdered?'

Her eyes glistened, and Emma wasn't sure if it was

because of her own mother's death or the morbid fasci-
nation of a teenager.

Fighting the urge to spin the girl around and
march her toward the village, Emma shook her head.
'No. Nothing like that. But I am responsible for your
safety, and it is time to return.'

As she spoke, a cloud drifted over, blanketing the
setting sun. The trees above quietened for a moment as
stillness gripped the air before fading as the breeze
increased, this time with a hiss as a whirly-wind whistled up the valley.

Emma shuddered and grabbed Zoe's arm in a vice-
like grip. 'Come on. We're going home.'

Zoe tensed under the pressure of Emma's grasp,
and Emma released her. 'Sorry, Zoe. I didn't mean to
startle you. Only it gets hard to see where we're going
once the sun's set—and we didn't bring a torch.'

Unsure if Zoe believed her lame excuse, Emma
lifted her chin and shortened Piccolo's leash, length-
ening her stride as they made their way home.

18

*Z*oe placed the final container in the back of the car before tucking a rolled-up towel around it to ensure it couldn't capsize.

Astounded at the variety of tarts her grandmother had made—apple, lemon, and blueberry—the lamingtons and cinnamon scrolls seemed almost superfluous. When she'd raised her eyebrows in question, Lola handed her yet another box and said, 'This is my annual contribution to the school. They support me all year with tuck shop orders and everything else. It's the least I can do.'

Zoe had nodded and trooped back to the car, once again laden with food.

After three days of blustery weather, leaden clouds, and frequent showers, the morning had dawned clear and bright, the air exuding that freshly washed feel, synonymous after rain.

Jittery with nerves as Zoe repeatedly reassured herself she was only singing with a bunch of kids—no biggie—she had busied herself that morning, rolling small squares of sponge cake in bowls of chocolate icing and perfecting the coffees for the numerous customers who'd descended on the town.

The private schools had closed for the year, allowing those without children in the state system to head off on holidays—and this year, more traffic than usual had passed through Featherwood Falls on the way to the coast, rather than join the queue of traffic on the highways.

A frazzled Frank returned from his mail run almost an hour later than usual, announcing half his recipients had been waiting at the box and considered it an excellent opportunity to share the latest weather report, cattle prices, and Christmas plans. Now he and Janet ran back and forth between the shop and post office, selling Christmas stamps, weighing parcels and, in their quiet moments, nipping through the adjoining door to assist Lola and Zoe in the shop.

The scents of coffee and pastries baking had filled the store since before seven in the morning and now, with the rush over and the car packed, Lola, Frank, and Zoe took a few minutes each to dress for the evening, leaving Janet to look after customers until closing time.

AFTER HELPING Frank and Lola transfer the food to the waiting trestle tables and gigantic fridges lined up along the back wall of the undercover play area, Zoe waved a hurried goodbye and darted toward the music room under the school building.

Despite the hint of damp in the enclosed concrete room, lights overhead burned brightly and excited children assembled in groups both inside and out of the small space.

'Zoe!'

Emma's voice echoed over the rabble, and Zoe raised an arm and wove her way through the children to reach her.

'Here's the program.' She waved an A4 sheet of paper at Zoe as two men pushed past them.

'Is this the piano you want?' One of them pointed to the portable keyboard tucked in the room's corner.

'Yes, please. Place it near the wall at the back of the stage area where children can't trip over it.'

Zoe grabbed the program and ran her eyes over the list. Beginning with "Principal's welcome and introduction", it detailed each year's presentation, the end-of-year awards, and last, the carols and Christmas songs to be sung.

Her head tilted slightly, Zoe met Emma's gaze with questioning eyes.

'I know. It's not there. That's because it's a surprise. We keep it that way so no one—or at least very few of us—actually know what will round up the event before everyone lets loose on the supper table.'

Zoe nodded silently, her stomach cramping again at the thought of standing in front of what appeared to be the whole town.

Emma rested a warm hand on Zoe's quivering arm. 'You'll be fine. We will both be fine,' she emphasized.

Without another word, Zoe followed Emma's instructions to help assemble the musical instruments in the appropriate place while Quinn, the principal, and Ashleigh, the second teacher, gathered the children into groups, stilling the excited babble.

As the sun spread a soft, afternoon glow across the playground, parents and visitors took their seats and Quinn tapped on the microphone.

Zoe sat in the back row beside Claire and Rhys, closest to the piano, and cast another glance around the crowd, disappointed that her father hadn't been able to get home in time for the concert. It had been three days since his last text, which had contained only six words.

Nearly done. See you on Saturday.

The evening seemed to crawl for Zoe. She'd had little to do with young children. After letting her mind dredge up cringe-worthy moments of end-of-year concerts, she tried desperately to recall the happy ones while the drone of Quinn's speech and the presentation of awards provided a haze of background noise. In the early years, her mother had attended every school function and Zoe had swelled with pride. Then, as Zoe hit puberty and hormones and pimples took over her body, she had withdrawn from all but the compulsory events, keeping a secret divide between her school activities and her constantly changing mother.

Following the various short skits each class had enacted, there was another rustle of voices and costumes as the students formed three lines—the tallest at the back and the first years at the front. Emma sat at the keyboard, an encouraging smile on her face as she nodded at Ashleigh, who had finally shuffled the last student into place.

Zoe stood, repositioning herself on the back wall and subtly conducting the anthology of Christmas carols and songs.

As they concluded and the parents clapped enthusiastically, Zoe moved to stand beside Emma's chair.

Quinn cleared his throat noisily and announced, 'Thank you, students. You may sit with your parents now, or here on the mat.' He pointed to a large rug that had been unrolled next to the stage. Whispers and rustling costumes accompanied the children as they dispersed. He waited until everyone settled before continuing. 'This evening, we have a new member of our community who is going to sing for us. Please welcome Zoe to Featherwood Falls.'

Necks craned and enquiring gazes met Zoe's as everyone clapped. In a second of frozen fear, she fixed her gaze on Claire and Rhys in the back row, holding her breath. Time stretched—her mind numb.

Emma whispered, 'It's okay, Zoe. You've got this.' She played the introductory chords, breaking the spell that had momentarily paralysed Zoe.

Swallowing the lump in her throat, Zoe opened her mouth and sang, quietly at first. As she focused on the words, her voice steadily rose, the pure, faultless notes silencing the audience. Zoe forgot everything around her as the lyrics and melody of the song consumed her every being. When she reached the chorus, she barely heard Emma's supportive harmonies.

She was that girl. The one who knew there was always going to be another mountain, another uphill battle. That sometimes she'd lose and it wasn't about how fast she got there or what was waiting on the other side—it was about the climb.

She reached the end, turning to Emma and meeting her smile. There was a split second of silence before the crowd erupted. Deafening applause was joined with shouts of "beautiful" and "well done". A loud whistle sounded from the back wall, and she grinned at Claire who had two fingers in her mouth, giving Zoe the same approving command she gave the dogs when they had excelled at their duties but were too far away for a pat or a quiet word of thanks.

In the rowdy aftermath, she didn't notice the man pushing through the crowd until he was in front of her, enveloping Zoe in an all-encompassing hug.

Stepping back, her faced suffused with blooming heat, Zoe yelped, 'Dad!' Only vaguely aware she had used the unfamiliar title for the first time, she whipped around to face Emma. 'This is my father, Emma. We weren't expecting him home until tomorrow.'

Zoe's smile faded at Emma's ashen face, her eyes wide and her hand clutching at her throat.

'Hi, Emma,' Ryan murmured. 'It's been a long time.'

Zoe swung her gaze from one to the other. 'You two know each other?'

'Yes,' Emma whispered. 'We do.'

'Of course,' Zoe muttered, frowning. 'You both grew up here.'

The school bell rang and Quinn announced, 'The formalities have now concluded, so let's celebrate the year we've had and enjoy this beautiful supper.'

Zoe linked her arm with Ryan's and turned him toward her grandparents, assuming Emma would follow.

Minutes passed as Lola and Frank welcomed their

son home and locals shook his hand, expressing their pleasure in seeing him again after so many years.

A spontaneous hug from Frank and the glow of having her father here while pulling off her performance, absorbed Zoe for long, satisfied minutes.

When she turned to find Emma, she had gone.

19

_H_eart pounding, Emma hurried along the road, her shoulder bag banging against her hip and her head bowed. She snatched the heeled shoes from her feet as she reached the corner, holding one in each hand, and ran the last hundred metres to her cottage. Then, taking the steps two at a time, she thrust the key into the lock with a shaking hand and slammed the door behind her.

Gulping mouthfuls of air, she leaned on the kitchen. Blood thumped in her ears as she perched on the stool, sprawled over the counter with her head on folded arms.

She didn't know how long she'd remained there. As the shock of coming face to face with Ryan and the subsequent blur of past hours cleared, the attention-needing yip of Piccolo penetrated her conscience. She sat upright.

'I'm coming Piccolo.' She slipped out the back door and released the dog with panicked hands, then followed the welcoming, writhing pup slowly back into the house.

What should I do? The words repeated again and again in her head.

As she had pushed past a group of parents talking with Ashleigh and Damian, Ashleigh had shot her a startled look, her forehead crumpled with concern. 'Are you okay, Emma?'

She had pressed a hand against her temple and mouthed, 'Not feeling well. Sorry.' Then she had fled with as much decorum as she could muster.

Collapsing onto the couch, she bent over, resting her elbows on her knees and kneading her forehead. *This can't be happening! Ryan is Zoe's father? But ... where, and who, is her mother? Where is the woman he brought to Featherwood Falls? Or ...*

Reality hit Emma with a bang, and she sat bolt upright. Was Zoe the "woman" who Ryan had brought home?

Her head spun. Heat crept up her neck and onto her face. Chiding herself for behaving rudely in front of the entire school community, she took slow, deep breaths before walking to the sink and filling a glass with water. As she sipped it, she replayed the past weeks over and over again. Zoe had turned up out of the blue. She had said she was staying with family. Did that mean Lola and Frank?

'Oh, Piccolo. What a mess. What should I do now?'

The dog tilted her head from one side to the other, slapping her tail against the floor.

Peering through the kitchen window, Emma stared at the silvery glow that shimmered in the garden. The sun had set and the full moon, although not yet visible from where she stood, threw a pearly light on the hills, bringing back memories of long ago when she had hovered on this exact spot, her heart hammering with anticipation and love—waiting, praying for her mother to fall asleep early so she could escape up the track to meet Ryan. It had always been ten o'clock at the junction. If either wasn't there, the other knew to wait an extra ten minutes then return home as something had caused the rendezvous to fail. These days, they would have sent a text to one another.

As the ache inside her eased, she wandered to her bedroom, stripped off her neat pencil skirt and blouse, and got into a pair of boxer shorts and a loose-fitting T-shirt.

She boiled the kettle and made a mug of camomile tea while Piccolo had a last run around the garden, then the two of them returned to the bedroom. Her stomach grumbled, but the thought of food almost made her gag. She reached into her bedside drawer and extracted a small photo album before flipping open the bright pink cover.

A slightly blurred picture of a young Emma and Ryan filled the first page. Ryan had his arm around her shoulder, and they were leaning into one another, blissfully unaware of the pair of pigeons crooning on the fence above their heads. The memory of that day came flooding back. It was summer, and they had spent the day at the local waterhole, swinging from the rope hanging from the huge rivergum on the bank, dropping into the deepest part of the pool and shrieking with laughter. Lola had packed them a picnic basket, and they had lain on the grassy bank, talking about their future while they chomped on salad rolls and light, fluffy apple turnovers. When they had arrived back at the store, Frank had been experimenting with the new camera Lola had bought him for Christmas and he had snapped the shot before they'd had time to change out of their swimmers.

A smile tugged at the corners of Emma's mouth. She wore a royal-blue one-piece swimsuit—her mother had severely disapproved of a bikini—a towel wrapped around her waist, and her long, blonde hair hanging over her shoulders in a wild mess. Ryan was in a pair of multicoloured board shorts, his broad, bare chest still wearing the red welt where the tree branch had slapped him. He had pushed himself off the bank with a massive spurt of energy, swung over the creek, misjudged the distance, and collided with the foliage instead.

That had happened only one week before he received his acceptance to university.

Emma flipped through the book, reminiscing as each photo brought a range of emotions, from happiness to despair.

She finished her tea and got up to brush her teeth then returned to bed. After switching off the light, she pulled the doona up and lay staring at the patterns dancing on the ceiling—the shadows of the tree leaves outside her window being ruffled in the moonlit breeze.

It was long after midnight when she gave up trying to sleep, wrapped herself in her winter dressing gown, and trod silently to the veranda. Curled up on the tiny cane sofa, she tucked a cushion behind her head and gazed at the hills. A boobook owl hooted from somewhere close by. What was the bird thinking. Did it have a mouse in its sight for supper? Or was it calling for its mate, feeling as confused and anxious as she was?

It felt like she had slept for only a heartbeat when she woke with a start as a wet, cold nose pressed against her cheek. She jerked upright, her taut body engulfed in terror before relief flooded through her. 'Piccolo. You gave me a fright.'

She glanced at the French door, slightly ajar. She couldn't remember if she had closed it. It seemed not.

Although Piccolo had been curled up in her bed when she'd wandered outside, it stood to reason she would have come looking for her mistress at some point.

Emma rubbed a hand over her face, lifting her gaze to the hills once more. Cast in moody shadows, their colours changed from dark purple to olive green as the glow of the rising sun spread across the horizon. She stretched the stiffness from her back and rolled her shoulders. Falling asleep in a scrunched ball on the tiny sofa had not been a clever idea. But as the memory of the previous evening returned, she took a deep breath and returned indoors.

AT NINE-THIRTY, three hours after she and Piccolo had returned from their morning walk, she hesitantly pushed open the shop door, her nerves fizzing. Swallowing her reserve, she gritted her teeth and approached the counter.

'Hello, love.' Lola greeted her with a wide smile. 'Sorry you weren't feeling too good last night. We missed you.' She wiped a damp cloth over the coffee machine as she continued, 'What a wonderful surprise you and Zoe gave us. That girl's got a voice like a canary, I reckon.' Lola puffed her chest out with pride.

Emma nodded. 'She sings beautifully.' She paused for a moment. 'I didn't realise she was your granddaughter—Ryan's daughter.' There, she had said it. Tension bit into her as tight as strings of a bow as she waited for Lola's reaction.

Lola's eyebrows shot up. 'Really! But didn't Zoe tell you? I mean, it was a shock for us too—probably not as much as it was for Ryan—but there you go. None of us knows what tomorrow will bring.' Lola paused, narrowing her eyes. 'Didn't Zoe tell you where she lived?'

Emma shrugged. 'No. I guess I didn't like to question her and ... well, you know, she's quite shy.'

The older woman leaned on the counter, lowering her voice. 'Poor mite. Her mum passed away, you know, and it seemed the only person who knew Ryan was her father, was Catherine.'

Emma frowned, confusion stealing her words. 'But ... how come?' She wasn't sure she really wanted to know but couldn't help herself.

A door slammed and both Zoe and Ryan entered the shop kitchen from the rear door.

Emma froze—like a deer in headlights. All thoughts of flight vanished in an instant.

'Hi, Emma,' Zoe said cheerily.

'Hi.' Emma's voice was low, the word guttural, as though she battled to get the single syllable to emerge from a frozen throat.

'Ashleigh told us you weren't feeling well and had to go home. I'm sorry. You missed a beautiful supper—

and everyone's congratulations.' Zoe smiled wryly. 'I didn't know many people, but they all seemed to know you and were pretty stoked with the whole thing.'

Emma's smile wavered, her resolve rapidly fading. Desperate to escape, she swung her gaze to the well-stocked shelves. 'I need to grab a few groceries.'

'Okay. See you later. Dad's running me up to Featherwood Station. I'm meeting Penny, another of Claire's pupils, and we're all going riding,' Zoe finished.

The doorbell jangled, and Lola touched Emma lightly on the shoulder as she greeted the heavily laden delivery man. 'Won't be a second, Emma. Gotta help this poor fella unload the bread.'

Zoe had disappeared, leaving Ryan poised at the door.

Their eyes met, and Ryan said softly, 'I'd love to catch up, Emma. Can I call in after dropping Zoe at the Shepherds'?'

Emma didn't trust herself to speak, her mind spinning. Noticing the lines that edged his deep blue eyes and channelled his tanned cheeks, she gave a brief nod, and he smiled then shot through the door, closing it with a bang.

Some things never change.

A grin flickered. Always as active and boisterous as a teenager, Ryan had banged all doors when he exited a room, leaving those behind suddenly bereft of his company—especially her.

20

*E*mma turned onto the familiar track and increased her pace. On reaching the cottage, Piccolo greeted her with enthusiasm, leaping up and down on the spot and crying in a desperate "I'm-so-pleased-you're-home" whine.

'That's enough!' Her waspish tone startled them both. She squatted and held the dog's head in her hands, rubbing behind the velvety ears gently. 'Sorry, Piccolo. Mum's a bit stressed at the moment.'

She opened the pantry and placed the yoghurt and cheese on a shelf. Then, turning to the fridge with a box of cereal in her hand, she huffed a sigh. 'Good grief, Ryan. Look what the mere thought of having you visit is doing to me.' Shaking her head, she switched the dairy products with the cereal and quickly emptied the grocery bags.

Darting into the bathroom, she brushed her hair and applied a coat of lipstick, staring at the wide, glistening eyes. She blinked rapidly. Her body flushed hot then cold as she worried about the upcoming meet-up. Was it due to anticipation? Or fear of reprisal.

Replaying the events of the previous evening, and those from long ago, her head bubbled like a cauldron. She returned to the kitchen and filled a water glass. Sipping the liquid slowly and practicing deep breathing brought a semblance of calm to her scattered thoughts—until the rumble of a vehicle pulling up outside sounded.

Her heart leapt.

Heavy steps trod onto the veranda and Ryan's solid, commanding frame filled the doorway. Haunting memories of their teenage love, followed by years of silence and separation, filled her with trepidation.

'Gidday.'

'Hi again.' Her voice tripped, and she cleared her throat. 'Come in.'

After slipping off his boots, he placed them beside the mat and stepped through the open French door, his socked feet silent on the polished wood.

Emma felt suddenly dwarfed. Although not a big man, Ryan had a presence about him she had not experienced in a long time. Wide shoulders wore his blue cotton shirt well, and pressed moleskin trousers hugged his legs. An internal smile wavered, imagining

Lola fussing over the laundry pile and ensuring all items were ironed and carefully hung in the wardrobe. Her gaze lowered, fixing on the large, work-worn hands dangling at his sides. Memories of her own small palm being encased in his paw, swinging at their sides as they walked, brought a lump to her throat.

'Coffee?' She forced her churning stomach to calm, determined to keep emotions in check, and walked behind the island bench dividing the kitchen from the dining area.

'Yeah. That'd be great, thanks.' Ryan's eyes swept around the room. 'You've changed things. It looks great.'

Emma tamped the coffee into the stainless-steel portafilter and clicked it into place on the machine. 'After Mum died, I renovated the cottage. Have a look around if you like—it won't take long.' A nervous giggle burst unexpectedly from her.

He smiled and peered through the doorway adjoining the living area and bedrooms. 'Nice. Clever idea to open up the hallway. Gives you a lot more space.'

The milk steamer hissed, and Emma didn't speak until she had poured the coffee into a mug and returned to the machine to make a second cup for herself.

'After Mum's hospitalisation, we installed a special bed in her room instead of that beautiful, timber-

framed one my father made before his and Mum's
marriage—but I kept it and now have put it back. Mum
couldn't speak for a while but I had no trouble inter-
preting her demands.' Emma snorted and Ryan's eyes
widened.

'Was she ... difficult?'

'Yes! The kind, caring mother I'd known vanished
for a while and became angry and demanding. After
she died, I had that wall removed, and got rid of the
box room at the end of the hallway to make the two
bedrooms and bathroom more spacious. So ...' She
shrugged, pausing for a few seconds. 'Now it's my
house and not my mother's.'

She met his wry grin. He didn't need to know how
much his letters and phone calls had lifted her spirits
during those hideous weeks of Maureen yelling and
throwing food. Throughout it all, Emma's thoughts
had dwelt on the stolen nights in the bush with Ryan
as she cleaned, cooked, and cared for her mother—
with the spasmodic help of a district nurse. When the
teacher's-aide position at Featherwood Falls had been
offered fourteen months after the stroke, Emma left
the house at eight o'clock each morning and spend her
day with the bright, inquisitive, and sometimes
mischievous school children. A life-saver for her.

'Shall we sit on the veranda?' Passing the mug to
him, she walked to the French doors before opening
the second one and hooking it back. A magpie sat on

the railing, warbling melodiously before flying away and landing in the flame tree in the middle of the lawn. Piccolo plonked herself in a patch of sunshine near the steps and lay her head on her front paws, her amber-coloured eyes roving from one human to the other.

Sitting in one of the two single chairs, Emma left Ryan the choice of the tiny sofa or the second cane chair. The tightness in her chest had eased, and she took several sips of coffee before lifting her gaze to meet his. 'So, you have a daughter,' she said as he lowered his well-muscled frame cautiously onto the sofa.

He rubbed his forehead before meeting her gaze with raised eyebrows. 'Yes. It was a shock. Got a phone call out of the blue from a solicitor. Apparently, Catherine had listed my name on Zoe's birth certificate—and had written a letter outlining our brief ... liaison. Not sure what would have happened if I'd changed my phone number. I'm sure there're hundreds of Ryan Browns in Australia, and I've lived in so many places both here and overseas. It might have taken a long time to find me. The phone number is about the only thing that hasn't changed in years.'

Emma finished her coffee and placed the empty mug on the small table beside her. 'You say it was a brief liaison. So ... not a loving relationship?' Heat flushed her cheeks 'Sorry. I don't mean to give you the third degree, but I'd like to know—if you're prepared to tell me.'

'It's okay, Emma. We go back a long way and I'm happy to share my past—or at least those missing years.' He paused, clasping then unclasping his hands as though unsure of where to begin. Clearing his throat, he continued, 'I'll be honest. There have been a few brief "liaisons", if that's what you'd call them, over the years. No one lasting—and no one I chose to spend my life with—least of all Catherine.'

Emma pressed her lips together. She didn't consider herself prudish, but, after Ryan, she had determined love to be hard won and something she wasn't prepared to pursue if the pain it caused was as unrelenting as Ryan's leaving her had been.

'I had no idea she was pregnant.' He shook his head. 'Wouldn't you think she would have let me know? Even if it was only for financial reasons? I would have been happy to help her—after all, I have never abandoned my responsibilities in the past.'

Her jaw dropped. A slow, rolling anger built deep inside her. A vein in her neck twitched. 'What about me?'

The lines around his mouth deepened as shock reflected in his blue eyes. 'What do you mean?'

Fighting the tightness in her throat, she swallowed, determined to contain her disbelief. 'I understood why you left Featherwood Falls—we'd both discussed that.

But we promised each other we would be together, even if we had to resort to letters and phone calls for a while. We believed our love would never die.' The last sentence was laced with anguish, and she paused, biting her lip.

Ryan leaned forward, a heavy frown creasing his forehead. 'B-but—it was you who said you didn't want to continue our relationship.'

This time, it was Emma's turn to be shocked. 'What on earth are you talking about?' she snapped. 'I wrote to you. Your mother gave me the phone number of your hostel and I phoned again and again, only to be told you were out and would call me back. You never did—and those letters you promised to write didn't last long, did they?' Her voice rose, and she took a shuddering breath as he cut in.

'Emma. That's crap! I wrote to you. Every week for months. I also rang this house whenever I could. Your mother always answered because you were NEVER at home! In the end, she told me you had asked her to pass on the message that our relationship was over and I was not to ring again.'

Emma leapt to her feet—her eyes wide and her heart pounding. 'Ryan. I would never do that. You know me—and you knew my mother. This is the twenty-first century. She wouldn't have said that ...' Her voice faded as memories of those horrendous few months following Maureen's stroke surfaced. Her mother had demanded the phone be moved into her bedroom where she guarded it possessively, insisting it was the only way she could remain connected to her friends now she was unable to drive. But, to refuse to allow her own daughter to talk to her boyfriend was both pathetic and selfish. She wouldn't have done that —would she?

Doubt crept into Emma's voice. 'The letters? We had no trouble exchanging them to begin with. It was the highlight of my day to run to the post office and collect those precious envelopes. It was only after I started working at the school that one of the ladies your mum organised to help would pick up our mail and drop it at the house—and that must have coincided with you deciding not to answer mine anymore.' She stopped suddenly, horror and humiliation trapping the sob that threatened to escape.

Could she ...? Would she ...?

Emma staggered, collapsing into the chair again. Was it possible that her mother had hidden, or worse still, destroyed Ryan's letters and fabricated the story of him wanting to end their relationship? This was the stuff of a Jane Austen novel, not that of a perfectly normal mother-daughter relationship in a friendly country town like Featherwood Falls. But why?

She froze. Had her mother known about their night-time meetings and decided to punish her? A wave of nausea rolled over her.

21

'*E*mma? Emma. Are you alright?'

She lifted her gaze to meet Ryan's as he leaned over her, one hand resting on hers.

With realisation crashing over her in heavy, repetitive waves, she drew a shuddering breath. 'Please believe me. I never wanted our relationship to end— and I never asked my mother to pass on any messages to you. I wouldn't do that. If something, or someone, had come between us, I would have told you myself.' She frowned at him. 'Did you ever ask your parents what was going on in this house?'

He nodded. 'Of course I did. Mum knew how upset I was. You know her, though. She would never interfere, and she liked and respected you too much to influence you.' His mouth clamped in a firm line. 'I never thought your mother would be that nasty, though.'

Emma heaved a sigh. 'Before she had that stroke, I wouldn't have thought so either. But something happened to her personality. She changed. Some days I hardly recognised her. She improved though ...' Her mind drifted and tears sprang to her eyes. Swiping at them with the back of her hand, she whispered, 'We never talked about it, and I didn't think she knew. But she must have. She was always so proper.' Emma looked up at Ryan. 'Remember how she used to skite to her friends when their kids were playing up at school or were caught smoking behind the tennis-court building that "Emma would never do that"? Then, when Lauren Masters got pregnant in grade eleven, she was mortified.'

Shrugging, she couldn't prevent the bitterness from colouring her words. 'Until it was me.'

Ryan knelt on the floor, keeping his hand on Emma's. 'What do you mean?'

She hesitated for a moment. The past was behind them. He didn't need to know. But something inside her thought otherwise. Enough lies had been told. Enough heartbreak had occurred and now she had nothing to lose. 'I was pregnant.'

He rocked back on his heels, losing his balance and toppling onto the floor. Piccolo leapt to her feet and rushed over, pressing her nose to his face. Scrabbling to stand again, he hauled himself onto the sofa. 'Pregnant!'

'Yes. I didn't know until weeks after you'd gone to Brisbane. It was soon after your mother and the other women started helping me here and I could get away. I took Mum's car and went to see a doctor in Stanthorpe. She confirmed my suspicions, and we talked about options. I was waiting for you to come home again so I could tell you. But ...' Her voice shuddered, and she met his soft, concerned expression. 'A few days later, I started feeling weird—and lonely. So, I walked to the hut while Mrs Stuart from down the road was here looking after Mum. I knew something was wrong. I lost the baby.'

'Oh, God. You mean you were up in the hut when you lost it?' Ryan ran a hand through his short, brown hair, leaving strands poking straight upright.

She nodded, shocked at the agonising moan emitted from Ryan's throat.

'I wish I'd known, Emma. How did you get home?'

'I waited until the cramping stopped and I felt better. The pain hung on and I was a bit of a mess, but I sneaked in the back door while Mrs Stuart was still here and had a shower before either she or Mum saw me.'

'I'm so sorry, Emma.'

Ryan lay a tender hand on her shoulder.

His touch sent long-forgotten sparks through her.

She yearned to be encompassed again in one of his bear hugs—the sort that made her feel as though an impenetrable blanket had laced her in a safe cocoon.

As though sensing her longing, his powerful arms wrapped around her, holding her with as much care as if she were made of porcelain. She leaned against his chest, the never-forgotten scent of Old Spice aftershave drifting up her nostrils.

They held each other for a long time, eventually drawing apart when Piccolo whined and pushed her way between them.

Emma looked down and smiled. 'Apologies for my possessive friend's behaviour. It seems Mum wasn't the only jealous one.'

Ryan grinned and glanced at his watch. 'I've got to collect Zoe from Shepherds' soon. There's so much I want to talk about, but I promised Dad I'd give him a hand to finish replacing that back fence. Can I come back tonight? Or tomorrow?'

Emma nodded, her face heating. 'If you want to.' Emotionally spent, she could barely think. But a warmth had seeped into her frozen soul and her shoulders sagged with relief. Now, except for the doctor, the one person who should have been first to know the truth did.

Meeting his affectionate gaze, she sucked in a long breath, grasping at Ryan's words and dragging her thoughts from the past. 'Zoe's welcome to bring you to our next music lesson. I'm sure she'd be happy to share what she's learned.'

'Thanks. I might do that.' He rubbed Piccolo's head as he traipsed down the stairs.

Emma followed and halted at the gate as he turned and hugged her again.

'See you soon.' Then he slid into the driver's seat, adding, 'She's a nice kid, isn't she?'

Emma nodded slowly. 'She's a beautiful girl, Ryan —and she's not a kid.'

He grinned, put the car into gear, and drove away.

She's a lovely girl—and she could have been ours.

22

_T_he door slammed behind Ryan as he strode away, his tuneful whistle bringing a grin to Lola's face. His departure left an emptiness in the room, but it was a good emptiness—much like the peaceful calm that never failed to wash over her as she locked the shop doors after a busy day.

Swatting the opportunistic fly that had come inside as Ryan left, she let her gaze drift to her husband, her head swirling with the conversation that had just taken place. 'So, what do you make of it all?'

'Geez, woman. I'm stunned. All these years we thought it had been Emma who called off the relationship. Did Ryan tell you anything at the time?'

Lola shook her head. 'Some. He was pretty upset, so I thought it best to listen without interfering. I remember being disappointed when he didn't come home for Easter that year—we both were. But we thought it was because of the work they had offered him.' She grunted. 'Those mobs paid him way more than we could afford, and we couldn't stop him from chasing his dreams. Turns out the poor lad must have been hurting more than we realised.'

'I s'pose. What a shame we didn't know the truth. We might have been able to help.' Frank ran a hand through his mop of white hair, scratched his unshaven chin, and placed the empty coffee mug on the cluttered occasional table. 'Mind you, remember what a hoity-toity witch Maureen could be? Pity help me if I put a Christmas card in her box that wasn't addressed properly. Anyone would have thought I was responsible for correcting her friend's spelling.' His voice quietened to a mumble. 'I felt sorry for Emma. Never could understand why she didn't just up and leave once Maureen was on the mend.'

Lola returned to the ironing board, hung the cotton dress on a hanger, and pursed her lips, a frown creasing her forehead. 'Maureen was a master manipulator. Makes my blood boil just thinking about how she deceived us all. Especially after the trouble we went to helping her out when she needed it most.'

She whipped a shirt from the washing basket, fiercely threaded it onto the pointy end of the board, and thumped the iron on the crumpled fabric. 'Fancy her not breathing a word about those letters. No wonder he was confused.' She shook her head, drew in a noisy breath, and huffed it out. 'What happened to those letters?'

'Love, it was twenty-five years ago. I can hardly remember what I did yesterday, never mind that far back. You know the routine. I guess I would have put them in her private box here in the post office—just like I did for everyone in town. It wasn't for me to study what they were or who they were from—or who collected her mail.' He paused, narrowing his eyes as if searching the depths of his memory for something —anything.

Shrugging, he spoke slowly, thoughtfully. 'I remember us talking about the suddenness of it all. When we moved here, we said we would never come between families in this small town. I know we've listened to lots of gossip and tall tales—seems to be part and parcel of being in business in a tiny town. But passing on that information is something we promised we would never do unless it was essential to life.' Frank sighed, lifting his feet onto the pouffe.

A dull ache wormed its way across Lola's left shoulder. After placing the iron on its stand, she switched it off at the wall and sat beside Frank.

He reached out and pulled her to him, resting his woolly head on hers, his hug easing the tightness that gripped her chest. She snuggled into his thin, wiry body, grateful for his common-sense reasoning and never-wavering support.

As the shoulder pain faded, a thread of hope fluttered in her belly. 'Wouldn't it be wonderful if they could pick up where they left off and find happiness with one another again?'

He squeezed her and kissed the top of her head. 'Ever the romantic. That's my Lola.'

She grinned and sat up straight. 'You know I get as much pleasure out of seeing others happy as I do from our own marriage.'

He rubbed his knees and hauled himself off the couch, pausing for a few moments while he straightened.

Concern filled Lola's eyes, and she stepped forward, wrapped her arms around him, and kissed him lightly. 'Those knees of yours playing up again?'

'It's nothing. Just getting a bit old for lugging these fence posts around, I suppose.' He chuckled. 'What do you reckon our chances are of getting Ryan to take over the shop for us?'

Lola stepped back in disbelief, a hand reaching out to touch the back of a chair to steady her frozen legs. 'What are you thinking, Frank? It's our shop and I'm not over the hill yet,' she snapped, immediately regretting her peevish reaction.

'Think about it, love. We're in our seventies and haven't had a holiday in over forty years. Don't get me wrong—I love it here, but you've gotta admit we can't keep doing this forever.' He planted another kiss on her head. 'Anyway, I'm going back to the paddock to finish the fence.'

She nodded silently, her whole body leaden. Every word he'd spoken was true, and that knowledge brought deep-seated concern she couldn't shake.

The shop bell rang, the distraction of Janet's murmurs penetrating the adjoining door and returning Lola's thoughts to her precious business. When they had arrived in Featherwood Falls, filled with determination and bright ideas of turning what was a worn-out country shop into a much-needed and appreciated general store and post office, they had worked fourteen-hour days and, with their little boy beside them, achieved every one of their dreams—and more. They had cleared the paddock behind the building of rusted, broken-down vehicles and shoulder-high weeds. A derelict shed, riddled with termites and rats, had quickly been dismantled—any suitable timber saved and sawn up for the home fire and the rest burned to a cinder in minutes.

Inside the shop, Lola had scrubbed and painted every surface and wall before restocking with an assortment of groceries. A long shelf had been erected, and each morning Frank had taken pride in organising the latest newspaper editions beside the scattered, subtly thumbed magazines. It had become clear quickly which were popular and which weren't, so adjustments were made and sales soared.

New benchtops and a stove had soon followed, and Lola turned the grotty alcove behind the counter into a sparkling kitchen where she could safely and efficiently produce fresh pies and patty cakes daily. The word had soon spread and, until the pandemic arrived, her baking drew customers from far and wide.

She took a deep breath, switching her thoughts to her granddaughter and Christmas. After returning from her riding lesson, Lola would suggest she and Zoe have a day in Warwick or Stanthorpe to do their Christmas shopping. Ryan and Frank could mind the shop while they had lunch at a café and gathered all they needed to make this Christmas one of the best.

Satisfied Zoe would jump at the chance of having a day out, she focused on the upcoming festivities and the shop. She would insist Janet have both Christmas Eve and Christmas day with her own family but would ask if she would mind helping on Boxing Day. It had been their tradition to open for two hours on each of the public holidays for locals to collect any last-minute items they may have forgotten. This year would be no different.

With her mind made up, she planted a smile on her face and entered her favourite domain—the kitchen.

23

Zoe gazed at her newfound friend. Until this morning, the opportunity for the two girls to meet hadn't eventuated, first because of heavy rain and then because, according to Claire, Penny had come down with a cold and her grandmother had confined her to bed. Although Penny was a year older than Zoe and approaching her final year of high school, the girls had quickly discovered their mutual enjoyment in riding, music—and the heartbreak of coping with parental issues.

'I promised Granny I'd help her tomorrow,' Penny said. 'We've got a Christmas party booked for Saturday and I said I'd be there to set everything up.'

As they had circumnavigated half the farm with Claire calling out instructions and giving a running commentary about the animals, trees, how the windmill-and-trough system worked, and a myriad of other farm-related information, the girls had also found time to exchange snippets of the how-and-why-we're-here scenario. Penny's tone had taken a bitter edge as she described her life attempting to achieve goals set by her parents—much like Natalia, Zoe had thought. Now Penny's parents had announced their plan to divorce. The shock had hit Penny like a sledgehammer and the bitterness flamed.

Uneasiness squirmed in Zoe's gut. She didn't want to hear any more. A vision of Catherine dominated her thoughts, and a wave of grief washed over her. Distracted by Penny's problems, her own enjoyment of the patchwork of fields, the rich black soil, and the kaleidoscope of crops and grasses was momentarily extinguished. Turning away from Penny, she gritted her teeth, relieved when the girl's next revelation was how kind her grandparents had been and how much Penny enjoyed living on Kallala.

During the minutes it took to wind their way through rough-barked trunks, temporarily blocking the vista below, Penny continued her seemingly essential synopsis of life on Kallala.

Although Kallala was only a small working farm, apparently the property's primary income came from the elaborate yet countryfied event facilities her grandparents had worked hard to achieve. Penny's description of the rambling five-hectare gardens—a large, glass-walled reception facility, a rustic chapel framed with wisteria, and a smaller timber-and-corrugated-iron shed that served as a workshop for all manner of art and craft—had Zoe's imagination running wild. To her, it sounded like paradise. Uncertain if Penny was exaggerating, Zoe kept her silence while they rode back to the stables.

Across the driveway, a cloud of dust signalled the arrival of a vehicle.

'Dad's here!' Zoe called, twisting in the saddle, one hand on the reins and the other on the horse's neck.

'Perfect timing.' Claire opened the stable gate wide and rode Akela to the railing before dismounting. After slipping the headstall over the mare's bridle, she turned to hold the girls' horses while they slid inelegantly to the ground.

'Good girl, Tango.' Zoe beamed at the horse, her face flushed with pleasure. 'Can we come again tomorrow, Claire?'

'Sorry, Zoe. I've got to finish a design project for one of my customers, so I'll need to spend the day in the office.'

'Oh.' Zoe's smile faded and, following Claire's instructions, she unsaddled Tango and carried the saddle to the tack room before picking up a brush and grooming the horse. Despite her reluctance to dwell on Penny's life and draw emotional comparisons to her own, her thoughts returned to the discussion about Kallala.

'Where does everyone stay?' she asked. 'Feather-wood Falls is not exactly huge—it doesn't even have a motel.'

Penny laughed, strolling past Zoe with Splash's bridle slung over her shoulder. 'Yeah, I know. We've got a bunkhouse set up in the shearer's quarters and fully equipped cabins scattered among the trees in the paddock near the homestead.'

'And if they run out of accommodation, we've got two farm-stay cottages now,' Claire added, lowering Akela's hoof to the ground. Besides learning to ride, she had also impressed on the girls how to care for a horse. Handling their hooves and ensuring they were clean of rocks and mud was an essential part of their care, and Zoe, in particular, took her responsibilities seriously.

Zoe stared at Claire in surprise. 'Where?'

'On the way to the woolshed.'

Straining to recall the building Claire was referring to, she could only picture the woolshed itself—a large, corrugated-iron building on timber stumps that edged the multiple small paddocks and yards near the creek. Then she remembered a smaller building shrouded by shrubs halfway between the homestead and the wool-shed. Perhaps that was it? The bushes provided privacy from the homestead and now she knew the building's purpose, she imagined it had spectacular rural views.

'They used to be our shearers' quarters, but Mum and Kirk converted them a couple of years ago. We don't get many guests over summer, but in the colder months it's surprising how many people from the coast come and stay. I reckon they love sitting around a fire and, even if it's a shock for them, those cold, frosty mornings are pretty special to see.'

'Hmmm,' Zoe replied slowly.

'Have you ever been in ice or snow, Zoe?' Penny's question was light and friendly but edged with a hint of superiority, reminding Zoe how little she knew.

She shook her head. In Brisbane, frost was rare, especially in the inner-city suburbs. The closest she'd got to ice was defrosting food from the freezer or seeing it in movies and Natalia's photos. The thought of crunching her boots along icy ground and having to crack the frozen water in animal troughs and bowls was, to her, fascinating but incomprehensible.

After giving Tango a last brush, Zoe walked over and gathered the assortment of grooming tools from the ground next to Penny. Straightening again, she twisted her mouth as a wry grin threatened. The top of her head barely reached Penny's chin. No wonder Penny had secured a place in her school's rowing eight. As the rower's arm muscles rippled beneath her skin-tight T-shirt, Zoe compared her own scrawny frame with the strong, lithe physique of Penny's. Even the thick, blonde curls swinging over the older girl's tanned shoulders brought a twinge of envy.

Her shoulders slumped as she removed the hair tie from around her wrist and scraped her own dark locks into a ponytail. A dog barked, and she looked up, the wave of self-deprecation fading rapidly as Ryan and Ginny approached.

'Hi, girls. How did your ride go?' Ryan said, the wide smile reaching his eyes.

'Great.' Both Zoe and Penny answered in unison, turned to each other, and laughed.

'They're doing well,' Claire added. 'Won't be long and we'll have them out mustering.'

'Well done, girls,' Ginny added. 'If you're finished, come and have a cold drink with us.'

Zoe's heart lifted. 'Thanks.' Ginny's friendly welcome reminded her of the congratulatory comments and praise the community had given her the previous evening.

I might not be an aspiring athlete, but at least my singing was appreciated.

Penny strode toward Ginny with a confident swagger, ignoring the three horses waiting patiently at the gate to be released. Catching sight of Claire's raised eyebrows, Zoe followed her gaze to Penny's retreating back, shot her a grin, and turned to unlatch the gate.

And I don't treat others like servants.

'DID YOU SEE EMMA?' Zoe asked Ryan tentatively as they drove away from the farm.

'Yes. I did. She was super proud of you last night—and so was I.'

Something in his tone made her fix her gaze on him. A worried frown stole across his forehead.

'And?'

He drew a deep breath, releasing his foot from the accelerator. The Prado slowed.

'It's a long story, Zoe.'

'I'm listening.'

'Emma and I have known each other since primary school. We were best friends—and boyfriend and girlfriend.'

'Oh.' Zoe's jaw dropped in surprise. 'So, what happened?'

Shrugging, he said simply, 'I stuffed up.'

'What do you mean, stuffed up? Did you cheat on her?'

'No, nothing like that. We really loved each other—at least as much as teenagers understand what love entails,' he added sardonically. 'Everything went wrong at the end of our final school year. Her mother had a stroke and Emma had to cancel her plans to teach in order to care for her. I left Featherwood Falls to go to uni in Brisbane. Things got kind of complicated from then on.'

'Oh yeah? Complicated—how?'

He looked at her, rolling his eyes. 'Are you sure you want to know all this?'

'Of course I am. I wouldn't ask otherwise. I really like Emma and now ... well, I kinda like you, too. So, tell me.'

'Hmmm, you can be quite direct when you want to be.' He grinned and heaved a sigh. 'They offered me work during the uni holidays, so I didn't come back here very often. I wrote to Emma—and phoned her—but, after the first few weeks, she didn't write back and the last time I rang her, I was told she didn't want to see me anymore.'

'Really? By whom?'

'Her mother.' He shrugged. 'Things were different then. We didn't have mobile phones and the further I got through my studies, the more holiday work I got in the mining industry. None of them were close by and ... well, I didn't come home to ask Emma why. I was pretty dirty about it—assumed she had another boyfriend. I finished my degree and moved to Western Australia. That's where I met your mother.'

Zoe nodded. 'You said. But if you and Emma loved each other, why didn't you follow it up at the time?' She recalled the romance novels that filled Mrs Worth's bookcase. Having secretly borrowed some, she had poured over them in bed at night before discovering other authors and genres. 'That's the sort of stuff that happened in books decades ago.'

'Because I believed her bloody mother!' He slammed his palm on the steering wheel, his shoulders drooping the moment the words were out.

'O ... kay.'

'Anyway, why didn't you tell Emma who you were? That you're my daughter and Frank and Lola are your grandparents?'

'She didn't ask.'

Ryan let out a noisy breath, pulled over to the side of the road, and braked. Meeting her gaze, he sighed. 'Sorry, Zoe. I shouldn't have spoken to you like that. I know you've been through more than most sixteen-year-olds. You have a right to privacy and, knowing Emma, she would have understood and not interfered. Lord knows she's done it tough, too.'

The corners of Zoe's lips lifted a smidgeon. 'So, are you going to ask her out?'

Ryan emitted a throaty chuckle. 'Early days, Zoe. But it's good to have things out in the open, and we'll definitely be talking more. We'll see what happens.'

Zoe grinned. 'Good. Maybe you could ask her to join us for Christmas? I like her.'

He glanced across at her. 'Actually, Ginny asked if we'd like to come to the farm on Christmas day. Your grandparents have celebrated with them since I left home—and regularly before that. There'll be a couple of others too—not sure who.'

As Ryan merged onto the road again, she clasped her hands together and stared through the side window. A thread of excitement wound its way steadily through her, a smile of hope creeping over her lips.

Perhaps Andrew will be there.

*a*fter placing the last bag of shopping in the car boot, Zoe slammed the door shut and beamed at her grandmother. 'I think we've got everything. It's been a lovely day.'

Lola brushed hair off her face and returned Zoe's smile. 'I reckon so. Let's get home now and see how the boys have coped.'

Frank and Ryan had willingly accepted Lola's plans. So while Frank had done the morning mail run, Ryan reassured them both he was quite capable of serving any number of customers and operating the coffee machine as if he had done it all his life.

Zoe turned the radio up as a playlist of familiar songs came on, and both she and Lola sang as they drove.

'I think Ginny and Claire will love their gifts, Zoe. It was very generous of you to think of them,' Lola said.

Zoe shrugged. 'They've been really nice to me, and I enjoyed shopping for so many people—especially now I have the money.'

Lola shot her a knowing grin.

Her grandmother was a generous employer, insisting she pay Zoe the standard hourly rate for a shop assistant with a Christmas bonus added this morning.

They both knew how difficult it had been for Zoe to have had no money to call her own and she appreciated the change.

'I've only had to think of Mum and Mrs Worth until now.' Her voice trailed off as sadness bit into her. An entire year had passed since then and her life had changed in ways she could never have imagined.

Lola released a hand from the steering wheel to rest it on Zoe's arm. 'I understand, love. We'd better get that parcel in tomorrow's post for Mrs Worth, or she won't get it in time.'

Zoe lifted her chin, brightening. 'She'll love the book—and that scarf. I don't think I've ever seen her wear anything really pretty. Her clothes are all so plain and boring.'

'She probably thinks your choices are the opposite.'

They laughed together and continued the banter as the silver sedan flew along the bitumen.

As they pulled to a halt in front of the garage, Lola leaned forward, a hand pressed against her chest.

'Nan! Are you alright?' Zoe's heart leapt at the sight of her grandmother's creased face and closed eyes.

For seconds, Lola said nothing but then drew back and gave Zoe a wan smile. 'That darn piece of chocolate cake I had for dessert must have been too rich, especially after the creamy pasta. It was delicious but I think my innards don't agree.' Brushing off Zoe's attempt to help her, she opened the door and slid out of the car.

'Hi, girls.' Frank's wrinkled smile greeted them as he reached out to take an armful of bags from both Zoe and Lola. 'Let me help.'

As he opened a large brown bag and went to peer inside it, Lola slapped his hand. 'Oh no you don't. You'll spoil the surprise.' Her tone was softer than usual, and Frank frowned, his attention jumping from the contents of the bag to Lola's face.

'You alright, love? You look peaky.'

'A bit tired. That's all. Town was packed.'

'Right.' Frank's face creased. 'You go straight in and put the kettle on. Zoe and I will bring everything in.' He nodded approval at Zoe as she gathered the last bags from the boot and slammed the door.

WITH PARCELS STOWED in cupboards and strewn over beds, the three of them sat at the table sipping tea while the tantalising whiffs of Thai chicken curry drifted around the room.

'Ryan's cooked dinner. You don't have to worry.' Frank placed his hand over his wife's. Their gazes met, and they smiled at each other. Zoe squirmed, feeling like an intruder.

'Thank you.' Lola whispered. 'We've only got two days until Christmas—and there's a lot to do.'

The door dividing the shop and home kitchens burst open and Ryan strode to the stove and stirred the curry. 'How was your shopping expedition?'

'Great. Nan and I had a good day, didn't we?' Zoe smiled, grateful for the distraction. 'We got masses of food for Christmas as well as ticking off the list of gifts —and we bought a heap of new decorations at half price.'

Ryan grinned at her, ruffling Zoe's hair as though she were a child. She reached out to slap him, giggling as he ducked and held the wooden spoon plastered with curry sauce toward her like a sword. 'I've invited Emma to dinner.'

Three pairs of eyes fixed on him wearing varying expressions of surprise and delight.

'I asked her to join us for Christmas as well.'

Lola opened her mouth to speak, but he shut her down and continued.

'Ginny wouldn't mind.'

'So … is she coming?' Zoe asked.

A playful smile. 'No. She's already accepted an invitation to join Maria and her family.'

'The Italian lady who works in the school office?' Zoe asked.

'Yeah. She and Emma have worked together for years now and are pretty good friends from what I gather. The Zillotti's have an orchard halfway between here and Stanthorpe—and an enormous family. Apparently, Emma's been joining them for Christmas since her mother died.'

Lola planted her hands on the table and pushed herself to standing. 'It will be lovely to have her here for dinner again. Just like old times.' Her round face once again wore a cheery smile, her cheeks pink and her eyes sparkling.

Zoe collected the empty cups and rinsed them in the sink while Ryan gave the curry another stir.

'I'll mind the shop so you can get organised here.' Before anyone objected, she disappeared through the adjoining door and closed it firmly as an unexpected wave of loneliness once again enveloped her.

WITH THE SHOP devoid of customers, Zoe grabbed a duster and worked her way around the shelves, wiping and tidying as she fought threatening tears.

It seemed everyone she knew in Featherwood Falls was happy. Even if, like Emma and Ryan, conflict and unreasonable interference had destroyed years of potential happiness, those days were gone. Except for her.

In a vortex of self-pity, she relived the death of her mother, the shock of discovering she had a family she'd never heard of, the disruption—and even possible destruction of dreams for a future in medicine. And none of that touched on the aching loss of city life with friends.

With the shelves finished, she snatched up a broom before sweeping work-boot clumps of soil, lolly wrappings, and a dead insect or two into the dustpan. Unable to mop the floors before closing time, she swapped the broom for the spray bottle of window cleaner and a cloth and began rubbing the massive panes of glass that faced the street. *Why me?* Frustrated love for her dead mother ripped at her. *Why did you let that mongrel into our lives?* She reasoned that, even at sixteen, she'd known the dangers lurking in the world of habit-forming drugs. Living in the city had at least provided her with an insight into a lot of things— homelessness, addiction, violence, and poverty to name just a few. How had her mother thrown away a hard-earned career, a nice home, and an amazing salary—all for a few hours of relief from the relentless slog and pressure her job had entailed?

By the time the windows gleamed and the sun had faded behind the hills, Zoe's frustration was spent and it was time to find the mop and bucket.

Voices sounded from the house as Zoe slipped out the front door and tipped the dirty water into the potted geraniums on either side of the worn, wooden steps. After locking the door behind her, she retreated to the cleaning cupboard beside the shop kitchen and stowed the equipment in the allocated position.

Opening the adjoining door, she startled as Frank loomed in front of her.

'Sorry, love. Didn't mean to frighten you.' He glanced over her shoulder and returned his gaze to hers with raised eyebrows. 'Have you locked up already?'

'Yep. And cleaned. It's ready for your inspection.' They exchanged a grin as she pointed to the tired-looking tinsel hanging in waves from one side of the store to the other. 'We can hang up the new Christmas decorations tomorrow.'

'You're a trooper. Thank you.' He patted her shoulder as he passed and headed toward the front to complete the evening closing.

Pleasure swept the last of her despair aside, replacing it with quiet determination.

If everyone else can find happiness in a tin-pot town like Featherwood Falls, there's hope for me yet.

25

*E*mma stepped out of the shower, dried herself briskly, and peered into the mirror.

Although butterflies swirled in her stomach, a new sense of anticipation heightened her usual pallor. Sparkling eyes stared back at her, luminous pools of blue, and she smiled, forcing her churning insides to calm. With the towel wrapped firmly around her, she picked up the brush and hair dryer and began styling her blonde bob, unable to keep the smile from her lips.

Half an hour later, clad in a pretty, above-the-knee-length dress—the soft, cool fabric sprinkled with tiny blue and mauve flowers—she swung in both directions in front of the mirror in her bedroom. Neutral-coloured sandals with the hint of a heel and a spray of tiny crystals glued to narrow straps encased her feet. It had been a long time since she had bought anything she considered "pretty". Years of maternal control and a tendency to want to blend into the background had ensured her wardrobe comprised smart trousers and skirts ranging in colour from black, navy, to grey, and were partnered with crisp white or pale blue blouses or polo shirts. Tailored jackets completed the outfits with, occasionally when the weather was colder than usual, a fine, high-necked woollen jumper.

'What do you think, Piccolo? Do you approve?'

The dog angled her head, listening intently, and Emma grinned. 'Come on then. You can have an early dinner tonight.'

She mixed the cup of kibble with pre-prepared mashed vegetables and a quantity of freshly minced beef. Then, with the excited puppy leaping around her as though determined to trip her, she placed the food in Piccolo's pen and latched the gate behind her.

'See you later, girl.'

Emma quirked a smile at the dog's lack of response. Bolting the food at breakneck speed appeared to consume one hundred percent of Piccolo's attention. After retreating inside again, Emma washed her hands and collected the bunch of flowers she had picked earlier. Then, popping her phone and house key into her shoulder bag, she picked her way carefully along the paddock track toward the store, her throat constricting with anxious anticipation.

WONDERING why she had got herself into such a tizz earlier, Emma relaxed, surrounded by old friends and new. Frank and Lola had always shown warmth and affection toward her but somewhere along the way— perhaps because of her mother's illness and Ryan's departure—she had felt the need to build walls around herself. Now she realised what a waste of energy and lost enjoyment that had been. She glanced at the half-grown joey hopping out of its basket in the room's corner. Nothing in this house had changed. It was still filled with as much love, loyalty, and chaos as it always had been.

Ryan flashed her a smile as she complimented Lola on the curry. 'I made it.' His tone was light, but she could tell he was pleased. 'I even made dessert.'

Remembering the days when the two of them would hover in the kitchen as Lola rolled, baked, and decorated the array of cookies, cakes, and tarts for sale —with Ryan sampling more than his share of the deli-cious products—Emma laughed aloud. 'You always said you didn't need to learn how to cook with a mum like yours.'

'Yeah, well. We all have to grow up some time,' he said with a poker face.

'What is it?' Zoe asked.

He stared at her blankly for a second. 'Oh, you mean the dessert?'

'Duh. Of course.'

He crossed the kitchen and pulled a tray out of the oven. 'An old favourite. Baked apples.'

Emma's eyebrows shot up. As children, they had sometimes helped—or hindered—Lola during apple season, preserving the cases of green granny smiths while they chomped on sweet, crunchy galas or a red delicious. Out of that experience had come the often-requested baked apples—their whole, round shapes cored and filled with dates, brown sugar, and cinnamon. Served with ice cream, it had become a staple in the Brown household—although in her own frugally governed home, according to her mother, dessert was not a course that a woman needed if she wished to keep her figure.

It was almost nine o'clock when Emma got up to leave. 'Thank you for such a lovely evening.'

Ryan jumped to his feet. 'I'll walk you home.'

Zoe shot him a knowing grin. 'See you in the morning. I'm off to bed.'

Walking hand in hand, the warmth of his palm enveloping hers, Emma turned toward Ryan, a soft breeze lifting her hair off her neck. Half of her wanted to tow him into a run, belting home to her cottage so they could spend the entire night together, wrapped in each other's arms like they had years ago. But the other half of her tugged the invisible rein, warning her to caution and think with her head and not her heart.

'You look so beautiful tonight,' he whispered. 'Just like you did ... back then.'

She raised her face to the horizon where a flash of lightning highlighted thick pillows of dark cumulus cloud. 'Thank you.' Her insides clenched. It was too early to let herself go. Making changes and promises hadn't worked in the past. What made her even consider it now?

'I-I can't rush things, Ryan.' Pain wiped the sense of contentment from her, her anguish returning. 'It's too early.'

'Hey. Don't worry. I know that. I'm not trying to push anything. I don't even know what I'm doing tomorrow, never mind in a month's time.'

Heat suffused her cheeks, and she drew a deep breath, grateful for the lack of streetlighting on her road.

'What does Zoe want to do? Will you take her back to Brisbane?'

'I honestly don't know. We've talked a bit. Agreed to have Christmas first then we'll discuss schooling and ... go from there I guess.'

'What about you? Continuing with fly-in, fly-out

work will make things difficult for Zoe.'

He shook his head. 'I'm not going back to that. It wouldn't be fair on Zoe, or Mum and Dad.' He paused for a few moments, rubbing a hand over his chin. 'To be honest, I got a shock when I came home. Mum and Dad have aged, and I guess I hadn't given their needs much consideration. Mum's not ready to give up the reins yet and I'm not sure I want to be a storekeeper.' He heaved his shoulders and sighed. 'The only thing I can think of is being with you.'

He halted and took both her hands in his. 'I know you need time, Emma. We both do. We were only teenagers the last time we were together and have been through a lot since. I've probably changed.' He grunted a chuckle. 'Hopefully for the better.'

'I know,' she murmured, her head bowed.

They continued to her front door, halting while she searched her bag for the key. After sliding it into the lock, she turned it and slowly pushed the door open, angling slightly, uncertain if he would follow her.

'Can I come in for just a moment, Emma? I won't stay.' He closed the door silently behind him.

Emma blinked. That was certainly a change. He could now shut a door without it being slammed.

Wrapping his arms around her, he kissed her gently on the lips. Her breath caught in her throat. Afraid to move in case she lost the tingling that enveloped her body, she pressed closer, long-forgotten passion igniting as their hands, lips, and hearts entangled.

At the exact second they were reaching the point of no return, a warning vision of Emma's mother's stern, disapproving face flickered above her. She froze.

His arms loosened, and he took a step back.

They stared into one another's eyes, hearts thumping.

'I'm sorry,' she said.

He nodded, rubbing gentle hands over her arms. 'I understand. Can I see you tomorrow? We can talk. Take our time.'

She gazed into the familiar grey eyes of the man she loved—had loved forever—and nodded.

He gave a small grunt, a smile hovering around his mouth. 'I'm not giving up. See you tomorrow night.'

With a quick, last hug, he shot her a cheeky grin, opened the door, and leapt down the steps before bounding into the darkness.

She smiled as he stopped to turn and wave.

Returning the familiar lift of an open palm, she remained on the top step for long minutes after his departure, breathing in the scents of fresh-cut lucerne and the heady, sweet fragrance of the night scented jessamine. In the distance, the ghostly hoot of an owl drifted in the warm, moist air.

Slowly, quietly, she closed the door and let the joyful wings of hope soar.

26

A bottle of wine followed the pot of tea as Emma and Ryan, hesitatingly at first, then willingly, as though desperate to unburden themselves of mistakes made, reflected on the years since the life-changing school formal.

'When I got that offer of holiday work in Western Australia, I thought it would be a great way of saving for us. For the future,' Ryan said, shrugging helplessly. 'Then when I came home, you were busy caring for your mother and those three days were all I had to see you. But helping Mum and Dad with the post office, mail run, and the shop took most of it. I should have ignored everything and everyone—except you.' He finished quietly.

She shook her head. 'No. You couldn't have. We

both had responsibilities ... and that was what had to come first.'

Their gaze lifted, meeting over the empty goblets. Ryan reached out and grasped Emma's fingers. 'I'm really, really sorry.'

She shifted from the chair opposite and sat close to him on the couch. Resting her head on his shoulder she heaved a long sigh. 'So am I.'

In silence, Ryan's arms encompassed her and they blended together as one. A gentle breeze rustled the leaves in the wisteria vine, while above, the milky way illuminated the darkness. They rose and made their way to the bedroom, Emma's playlist beginning the loop again, softly serenading them with the soundtrack from "The Man from Snowy River".

Her last thoughts as she kicked the door shut were of the unintentional but blissful accompaniment as the lonely, heart wrenching twenty-five years without each other, melted away.

It was Christmas Eve, and the shop kitchen was warm while the store heaved with the tantalising scents of gingerbread and fruit-mince tarts mixed with freshly ground coffee.

Emma drifted past the magazines as though carried by a set of wings or some sort of silent helicopter—the result of Ryan's arrival at her cottage at eight o'clock the previous evening and his departure as the golden glow of sunrise had spread over the horizon.

'Hi, Emma.' Zoe popped her head around the display cabinet, a knowing grin plastered across her face. 'Have a good night?'

Heat crept up Emma's neck, and her mouth dried suddenly. She swallowed as their eyes met.

'Don't worry.' Zoe dropped her voice to a whisper. 'I reckon it's cool. You and Dad together again after all these years.'

Relief flooded Emma, sweeping the remnants of hesitation away. 'Thanks, Zoe. I'm pleased you approve.'

Zoe blinked. 'Why wouldn't I? You're a pretty cool lady and my dad's not too bad either.'

Emma almost choked as a distinctly unladylike snort escaped from her.

'Are you looking for something?' Zoe continued. 'Nan's having a little rest, so it's just me here.'

A frown creased Emma's forehead. 'Is Lola okay?' She had never known Lola to rest during the day— although, until this past few days, it had been several weeks since she had enjoyed a proper chat with her.

'I think so. She's been up early again though, so she's probably tired.' Zoe swept her gaze over the containers lined up along the benchtop. 'Baked these while I fed the animals, then we wrapped Christmas presents together while Pop looked after the shop. He's next door if you want to see him. Dad's off doing the mail run.'

A little surprised to hear Zoe refer to Frank as Pop, Emma gave a small nod of approval at Zoe's succinct report of everyone's whereabouts. It was another step in this horrendously emotional journey for a sixteen-year-old—but a good one.

'I thought I'd pick up a couple of large bottles of lemonade and some of those fresh cheeses Lola was telling me about. I'm having the day at Maria's tomorrow, and she's such a fabulous cook I never know what to take.'

'Sure. Grab whatever you need while I duck out the back and check on Nan.'

Flashing Zoe a smile of acknowledgement, she then turned toward the dairy fridge. After trying to decide which of the five new cheeses to purchase, she gathered one of each as Zoe returned—the kitchen door announcing her arrival with a bang and immediately bringing back memories of Ryan's habits and of the previous, deliciously exhausting night with him.

'Emma!' Zoe's voice was high-pitched with anxiety. 'Something's wrong with Nan. Can you come?'

Emma dumped the cheeses back into the fridge and rushed through the kitchen behind Zoe, almost treading on her heels. Emma's consternation grew as they crossed the living room and hurried down the hall to Lola and Frank's bedroom. She had never, ever, been in Ryan's parents' bedroom.

Lola was half-sitting on the bed, propped up by pillows and hugging a rug to her chin, her face grey and clammy.

'Lola! What's the matter?'

'I'm sure it's nothing. Just a bit of indigestion—and tiredness.'

Although aware of her lack of medical training, Emma's own mother's illness had opened her eyes to many more health issues than she cared to know about. And while Lola was obviously attempting to dismiss her discomfort, fear and pain was etched on the older woman's face.

Emma leaned over and pressed the back of her hand to Lola's damp forehead. Shallow, gasping breaths lifted and filled the hollow at the base of Lola's throat, accentuating pale skin and dark, throbbing veins.

'Where did you say Frank was?' Emma shot a worried glance at Zoe. The last thing she wanted was to frighten her, especially given the recent trauma of her mother's death.

'In the post office. He said he wanted to have a tidy up now the Christmas parcels and mail have been delivered.'

Drawing a deep breath, Emma spoke calmly.

'Would you run and get him please? I think it's wise we call an ambulance.'

Zoe's eyes widened, reality and horror rendering the girl immobile.

Reaching out, Emma grasped her arm. 'It's probably nothing, Zoe. I might be overreacting. Only we're a long way from the nearest hospital, and with Christmas it's best to get the problem seen to as soon as possible.'

Face chalky, Zoe nodded, spun around, and fled.

Emma summoned the ambulance, advising them of the details and stopping frequently to listen to the questions being fired from the other end of the phone before answering.

Zoe and Frank arrived within two minutes, a wild look of disbelief in the old man's eyes. He rushed to Lola's side, clasping her hand between both of his.

Emma swung her gaze from Zoe to Lola and Frank, keeping her voice low and drawing on years of experience with children. They needed to know the truth—and the risks. 'I'm not sure, but after talking to the paramedics, we're wondering if something's not quite right with Lola's heart. The paramedics are on their way—and I'm sure they'll take a lot less time getting here than we do when we go to town. Frank, would you mind helping me get Lola into an upright position? It's important she sits up straight—then we need to pack a bag for her in case the hospital wants to admit her.

Zoe, please ring Janet and ask her if she could come and give you a hand in the shop.' She glanced at her watch, willing Ryan to walk through the door. 'When do you expect Ryan home, Frank?'

He stared at her blankly, as though the scene unfolding in front of him was a best-forgotten nightmare—or a drama-filled movie. Then he shook his head as though to clear the fog. 'Not for another hour, possibly longer. He had a full load today and lots of people will expect him to exchange good wishes and who knows what else.'

'Okay.' She turned to Lola, sharing an encouraging smile as she slid an arm around her shoulders. 'Come on, my friend, let's get you more comfortable.'

Zoe snatched her phone from her pocket. 'Do you remember Janet's number, Nan?'

Lola pointed to the diary on her bedside table. 'Front page. Phone numbers,' she whispered.

Zoe punched in the digits and moved to the hall to talk.

Frank's gaze followed her out the door and he cast a worried look at his wife. After snatching an overnight bag from the wardrobe, he plonked it on the floor and, in a shaky voice, rasped, 'What do I pack?'

Within minutes, Emma was satisfied they had Lola sitting as directed by the woman on the other end of the ambulance call, encased in a bright-pink dressing gown and slippers. Hastily helping Frank assemble items of clothing, toiletries, her mobile phone and charger into the bag, she paused, her eyes sweeping the room. 'Your medical cards, Lola. Are they in your purse?' She pointed to a handbag hanging on the wardrobe door.

Lola breathed a soft, 'Yes', and Emma removed Lola's well-worn leather purse and dropped it into the overnight bag before zipping it firmly closed.

'Now your turn, Frank.'

'Why do I need to pack stuff?' He brushed a hand through his hair, shaking his head in bewilderment.

Emma lay gentle fingers on his arm. 'You'll probably go in the ambulance with Lola. She'll need you and so will the staff when you get to the hospital. You will be Lola's voice if she's not up to it.'

For a second, his faded blue eyes shimmered with unshed tears.

She turned away, glancing into the open wardrobe and running her eyes over the top shelf. A battered leather suitcase sat in the corner. 'Can you get that down please, Frank? We'll pop a few things into it for you.' As she spoke, Zoe burst through the door, announcing Janet was on her way.

'Thanks, Zoe. Would you try ringing your dad, please?'

While dark hair hung over Zoe's down-turned face, Emma adjusted the pillows around Lola and rested a reassuring hand over Lola's. 'Won't take long. The ambulance is on its way, and you'll be in the hands of the doctor in no time.'

Frank shot a worried glance at them both as he jammed a clean pair of jeans, a handful of underwear, socks, and two shirts into the suitcase.

Zoe huffed. 'Straight to message bank. He must be out of range.'

'It's okay, Zoe. Perhaps you could go out the front. Keep an eye out for the ambulance and Janet and keep trying your dad.'

Zoe nodded and hesitantly backed out of the room.

'Frank, would you mind sitting with Lola? I'll make sure the back door is open and the path is clear for the paramedics to bring their gear in. It'll save time once they get here.'

He nodded, shuffling closer to Lola and holding her hand in both of his.

It felt like hours to Emma as they waited. She imagined the ambulance rocketing around corners and speeding along the straights with lights flashing and the siren screaming.

'I'll need the car,' Frank said randomly. Both Emma and Lola stared at him as though he had said he needed to climb a ladder.

Taking a moment to zone in on how Frank was probably thinking, she said, 'It's okay, Frank. As soon as the ambulance has collected you both, I'll nip home, get my car, and follow. By then Janet will be here and

Ryan shouldn't be far away. We can make more plans once we know what's happening.

'Should have got Rhys to escort us and driven into town ourselves. That's what we should have done,' Frank muttered.

Emma bit her lip. 'The lady on the phone was very firm about that. She said we were not to drive her. It wouldn't be safe. If something happened to Lola on the way, neither you nor I would know what to do. Anyway, although it might take us an hour to get to town, the ambulance will make it much faster,' she finished, her comments laced with far more confidence than she felt.

'The ambulance is here!'

As Emma had predicted, Zoe's yell echoed through the living room forty minutes after Emma had placed the call.

'Stay with Lola, Frank. I'll bring them through.' Emma dashed out the door, meeting Zoe in the hallway.

'What shall I do?' Zoe's voice cracked with despair.

Emma grasped her hand and towed her outside, whispering reassuringly to her, 'It's okay, Zoe. They're here now and will take care of Lola.' To distract her, she asked, 'Is Janet okay in the shop?'

Zoe nodded. 'No answer from Dad yet, though.'

'He'll be here soon.' Emma switched her gaze to

the two paramedics coming toward them, loaded with bags and equipment.

'Hello, ladies,' one of them wearing a name tag displaying "Paul" said.

Zoe and Emma turned instantly, hurrying back inside as the paramedics followed.

While Paul applied an oxygen mask to Lola's face, another paramedic eased Lola's clothing aside to connect electrodes to her chest, arms, and legs. Then they pressed the button and the multicoloured screen sprang to life.

After slipping a needle into Lola's arm, Paul connected an intravenous line. 'How's the pain out of ten? Now the real score please, no heroics,' he said with a wink.

'Nine.'

'We can't be having that, can we? We've got drugs to help. Any allergies?'

Responding to her shake of her head, he smoothly injected into the line, watching as Lola's face relaxed and her breathing became less laboured. His colleague read the squiggly lines on the monitor and confirmed their suspicions. 'Wee bit of bother with your ticker, love. We're glad you called us. Just one or two minor adjustments before we take you off for a ride, Lola. Pop this aspirin under your tongue.'

While Lola obeyed, Paul explained they would talk

to their senior advisors from the ambulance—who would direct them to the most appropriate hospital.

Minutes later, Lola was installed in the ambulance and Paul gave Frank a reassuring smile, inviting him to accompany his wife for her ride.

Frank shot a bewildered glance at him. 'The bags? Can I take them with us?'

'Of course.' The second medic smiled at him, ensuring Frank was buckled in and the gear stowed securely before climbing in to take a seat beside Lola.

Paul closed the doors as Emma called out, 'I'll follow in my car and meet you at the hospital.'

As they drove off, Emma gave Zoe a quick hug. 'I'll just nip home and get my car. You wait for Ryan and ring me when he gets home. We can talk while I drive —provided we are in range.'

Then, without waiting for Zoe's reply, she snatched her shoulder bag from the lounge sofa and ran.

THROUGHOUT THE DRIVE Emma fought the memories of a similar, horrific journey she had taken twenty-five years earlier. The shock. The pristine, disinfectant-fragranced hospital. The hustle of staff as they'd readied her mother for transfer to Toowoomba. An inability for either of them to speak, Maureen because she couldn't and Emma because of mind-numbing fear. Squashing those thoughts, she focused on Zoe, dearly wishing she had stayed with her but knowing that Frank and Lola needed her more. Although ... she reflected on the girl's reactions, surprised to have noticed a calm acceptance of the situation and a surprising maturity once the initial shock had settled. She glanced at her watch.

Ryan should be home by now. Why haven't they called?

Checking in the rear-vision mirror, and satisfied no one was behind her, Emma pulled into the next available farm entrance and picked up her phone, relieved she had two bars of reception. Then she punched in Zoe's number.

'Emma! Is everything okay?' Zoe's voice was high-pitched, and Emma could feel her anxiety.

'So far, everything's going as planned. Once I reach the hospital and I know what's happening next, I'll ring you again.'

'That's good ... I think?'

'Is your dad home yet?'

'No. But I got hold of him a few minutes ago and he said he'd be back within half an hour. Janet's here and the shop has quietened down, so we're okay.'

'Thank you, Zoe. You're a trooper.' Emma's shoulders sagged with relief.

'Don't worry about Piccolo—or anything. I'll feed the animals here then go to your place later on if you tell me where the key is. Hopefully, by then you'll know more.'

'Thanks, Zoe,' she shouted as an opposing truck whooshed past, rocking the car in its turbulence. She shared instructions on where to find the key before adding, 'I'd better get going now. I need to be at the hospital when the doctor sees Lola. Talk again soon.'

After pressing the red icon, she dropped the phone on the passenger seat, flicked her indicator on, and pulled back onto the road.

What an amazing girl.

27

Zoe's head buzzed with worry and past images. Determinedly, she forced her fears aside, convinced that no one, not even God would take her newly discovered grandmother from her. She scooped another dipper of pellets from the dark steel drum and poured it into the bucket. *Repeat and tip—* she counted the scoops then lugged the trugs into the kangaroo paddock before dividing them equally between the containers. Newly weaned and aged wallabies and eastern grey kangaroos jostled for position at the feeders. Lifting her gaze, she grinned at the row of hand-reared-and-now-weaned macropods lined up near the back gate. Waiting until the weaker animals had eaten, she jogged up the rise and threw the gate open.

After closing it securely behind the last creature, an

arthritic buck with torn ears that had passed through into the safety of the night paddock, she followed the track running parallel to the fence, reaching Emma's cottage within minutes.

A jubilant Piccolo leapt in the air, her delight at seeing a friendly face demonstrated with excitable, high-pitched yips.

Following Emma's instructions, Zoe released the dog from her pen, allowing her to race in circles around the house while she located the back-door key, entered the cottage, and collected the leash.

For the next thirty minutes, the two of them ran— along the lower track, up the bitumen road toward the hills, turning right onto the narrow strip of gravel adjoining the top and bottom roads of the valley, then back toward the village along the main road.

Waiting, waiting, waiting.

Zoe panted the word as she jogged, certain that no news was good news—just as Mrs Worth had said a million times when Zoe's mother hadn't arrived home at the expected time.

Puffing and with shins burning, she slowed to a walk as she and Piccolo crossed the bridge. Allowing herself a few seconds to stop and lean over the railing, she revelled in the sense of peace that never failed to fill her as the water tumbled over the rocks. The charcoal cumulus clouds that had threatened earlier in the day had cleared, leaving only a few strata white-washing the backdrop of blue.

Her phone rang as they turned for home, its raucous ringtone startling both Zoe and the dog.

'Dad! What's happening?'

'They have flown her to Brisbane. They reckon she's got a blocked artery going to her heart, so they'll be taking her to the cath lab as soon as she arrives for tests and a confirmed diagnosis.'

'Oh my God, that sucks. Will she have to have surgery?'

'From what the hospital said, heart stents are a less invasive and wonderful way of helping patients now but we won't know until she's been seen. Hopefully, if their suspicions are correct, they'll insert the stent and send her home again in a few days.'

A relieved huff seeped noisily from Zoe's throat. 'That's good. Where are Frank and Emma?'

'Frank wasn't able to go in the helicopter, so Emma's driving him to Brisbane now and I'll talk to her after they arrive.'

'I'm nearly back to Emma's with Piccolo. Be home soon.'

'Okay, see you then.'

It was only after she slid the phone back into her pocket that she realised what she had said. *Dad,* not Ryan.

Zoe was carefully measuring Piccolo's food into her dish when her phone buzzed. She jumped, snatching it out of her jeans pocket and spilling kibble on the floor.

Juggling the phone at the same time as attempting to scoop up the spillage with one hand, she swiped the green icon without looking. 'Hello, Dad?'

A slightly bemused female voice replied, 'I'm not Dad. It's Claire.'

'Sorry, Claire.'

'What's up? Have I caught you at a bad time?'

'Not really. Well, kind of. Lola's sick and Emma and Frank have taken her to the hospital. Well, the ambulance did really.'

'Whoa! Slow down. Tell me everything.'

At the sound of Claire's concerned but calm request, Zoe poured out the events of the previous hours. '... so now we're waiting to hear how the surgery goes.'

'Where's Frank now? And Emma?'

'They're on their way to Brisbane to be at the hospital with Nan. Emma's driving.'

'Good. And where's Ryan?'

'Back at the shop. With Janet.' Zoe frowned at Piccolo as she gobbled up the last of the spilt kibble then shrugged. What did it matter if the pup broke the eating-before-being-given-the-command on this occasion? There were far more important issues to worry about.

'Okay,' Claire said. 'I was actually ringing to suggest you bring your swimmers tomorrow. We thought we'd go to the falls for a swim after lunch. But now ...'

'Cool. That'd be nice—except, I don't know what we're doing now?'

'I know. Let me have a talk with Mum. Then we'll nip down and work out how we can help.'

Zoe's shoulders sagged as the load of the day's events suddenly lightened. Ginny and Lola had been friends forever and the relief of having to stay strong, as she had following her mother's illness, was a struggle. 'Thanks, Claire. See you later then.'

'See ya.'

After sliding the phone back into her pocket, she spooned meat onto the remaining dry food in the dog dish and headed out the back door.

'Come on, Piccolo. I'm sorry, girl. You'll have to go back in your pen for a while. Emma will be home tonight—even if it's really late.'

Her mouth twisted as soon as the words were out. Would she? An emptiness returned to her, reminding her of the loneliness and desolation that had consumed her for days following Catherine's death. If Lola didn't pull through, would Frank feel the same? Would Ryan?

She shook herself, latched the pen, and jogged back to the store.

FORKING Ginny's delicious spaghetti bolognaise into her mouth, having given up all attempts at eating both carefully and with decorum as it had been hours since any of them had last eaten, it took Zoe a few seconds before she felt satisfied enough to concentrate on Ryan's story.

'She's out of theatre and everything is going well. Emma's going to get Dad booked into a motel as close to the hospital as possible and then come home. I'll grab a couple of hours sleep while we wait for Emma to get back safely, then I'll drive to Brisbane so I can be with Dad overnight and we can go to the hospital together tomorrow.'

'What do you want me to do?' Zoe wiped her mouth on a napkin, her voice tight with emotion. Half of her wanted to be with her father and grandparents, her newly discovered family too precious to be parted from. The other half wanted to prove she was stronger and more reliable than any of them realised—and perfectly capable of taking care of the shop and animals.

'You're coming home with Kirk and me,' Ginny said firmly. 'We'll take Pixie with us and bring you both back in the morning.' She pointed to the little kangaroo who had escaped her sleeping bag and was now hopping around the room. 'Claire and Rhys will nip down and give you a hand to feed up here, and then you'll all come back to the farm for the day. Lola likes to open the shop for two hours on Christmas Day to keep the locals happy and Janet said she will take care of it.' She paused; her head tilted. 'Sound, okay?'

Christmas. Of course. With the drama of the day, Zoe had almost forgotten. Her own family wouldn't be with her, but Ginny, Kirk, Claire, and Rhys would.

'Sure.'

Disappointed Emma wouldn't be joining them, it satisfied her knowing that at least she would have an enjoyable day with Maria and her family. Ryan would be with Lola and Frank, so none of them would be alone.

Christmas would not be as she and Lola had planned, but at least they had shopped for food. Her thoughts flicked back to her grandmother bent over the steering wheel after arriving home.

Poor Nan. She must have been feeling unwell, but she never complained.

Anxiety wasn't far away; after her mother's admissions, Zoe knew all about hospitals, with their shiny floors, bright lighting day and night, and all the beeps and smells. She shuddered at the memories.

SNUGGLED under a warm doona in the guest bedroom of Featherwood Station, Zoe lay staring through the window at the night sky. Shimmering dots peppered the blackness while swirls of white trailed through the Milky Way. In the city, stargazing bore no resemblance to what she saw out here. Distracted by streetlights, vehicles, and soaring multi-level buildings, getting a clear view of the world above was a challenge. Contemplating getting out of bed to search for the Southern Cross, she decided against it as a chilly breeze wafted through the room.

Zoe felt safe and loved. Surprisingly so, given those she had met since arriving in Featherwood Falls a few weeks ago hadn't been there when things went wrong in her life. They knew only what they had been told—and Zoe doubted they really understood. Still, they had welcomed her like family, and now with the events of the day replaying over and over in her mind, her heart was full.

The old house creaked as the wind blew through the trees, rattling the French doors along the veranda. It was Christmas Eve. She glanced at the bedside clock. In seventeen minutes, it would be Christmas Day. A day to be celebrated and embraced—and her first Christmas without her mum.

Picking up her phone, she reread the message from Ryan—sent only thirty minutes earlier.

Nan's awake but groggy. Doctor's happy and positive about a good recovery. At the motel now with Dad. Talk in the morning. Love you, Dad.

She yawned. Warmth and exhaustion wrapped her in its arms, and she closed her eyes, the hint of a smile touching her mouth as sleep claimed her.

ola's muddled head gradually cleared as blinding light and muffled voices penetrated her consciousness.

Her nose itched, and she moved a hand to scratch it, catching her fingers against a tube. She suddenly remembered where she was—and why.

Hospital.

A chair creaked, and Frank's familiar face loomed above hers. 'Hello, love,' he whispered. 'Merry Christmas.'

A smile touched her lips while rhythmic beeps gave reassurances of a steady heartbeat. As her vision cleared, she took stock of the tangle of tubes, flashing lights on the machine next to her, and the nurse hovering on the opposite side of her bed from Frank.

'Good morning, Lola. Merry Christmas.' The

woman spoke in a chirpy voice as though she had not a care in the world.

'Hi,' Lola rasped, her throat dry and rough.

'How's the pain level out of ten?'

Lola took a deeper breath, feeling a tightness some-where in her chest but no discomfort. 'There isn't any,' she said with surprise. The jaw and shoulder niggles that had plagued her for weeks appeared to have gone.

'Perfect. I'll just do your obs, and we'll organise some breakfast for you. How does that sound?'

Lola blinked. A vague memory tugged at her—of being wheeled on a trolley and people bending over her, lifting her from one hard bed to another. Someone —a tall man of around Ryan's age and wearing pale-blue scrubs and a face mask—had murmured some-thing to her, but she couldn't remember what he'd said. Then, her head thick with grogginess and a leaden body weighing her down, she had drifted into darkness, leaving no memory of anything, not even a nightmare, until now.

She turned her head toward Frank. 'What time is it?'

He grinned, grasping her hand gently in his. 'Quarter past seven on Christmas morning. They put a stent in your blocked artery, and you've had a good night, apparently.'

Her face clouded, her eyes struggling to focus. 'Where did you sleep?'

'Don't worry about me, love. Ryan and I had a nice little hotel room just down the road. Ryan's gone to have breakfast while I sit awhile with you, then we'll swap.'

She frowned. 'How's Zoe?'

'She's fine. Ginny took her to the farm. Ryan will give us an update when he arrives, but you know Ginny will make sure she's okay. Anyway, you'll be home again in a day or two, so you'll be able to see for yourself how capable Zoe is.'

Lola gave a tiny nod.

The nurse leaned over, a smile widening the thin, olive-skinned face. 'Yep. We don't do discharges on a public holiday and the pharmacy will be closed until the day after Boxing Day. But by then, you'll be up and running.'

Lola swung her gaze back to Frank. 'Will you stay with me?'

His face softened as his blue eyes met hers. 'Of course I will. I can't sleep with you yet,' he shot her a cheeky wink. 'But I'll be here all day unless they kick me out.'

'Doctor will be here shortly and, if he's happy with your progress, will give us the go-ahead to remove some of these tubes. This afternoon, we'll transfer you into the ward where your family can visit. They can spend the day with you if you want them to.' The nurse scribbled on the sheet of paper attached to the clipboard as she spoke, a knowing grin on her face. 'Unless you want to have peace and quiet. Call it a retreat, perhaps?'

A silent chuckle burbled in Lola's throat. It had been many years since she had last been a hospital patient, but whenever she visited a friend in a comparable situation to the one she now found herself in, peace and quiet had been non-existent. Tea trolleys clattered, uniformed staff swished in and out of the rooms, and buzzers and phones rang constantly. And that racket didn't include the moans of demanding patients in the rooms across the corridor or the hushed, and not-so-hushed, conversations between visitors and medicos as they rushed up and down the linoleum-floored hallways.

She drew another deep breath and released it slowly as she stretched out her fingers and toes. There was nothing else for it except to do her utmost to obey doctor's orders and ensure she qualified for discharge the moment she could.

MINUTES LATER, Ryan appeared, then the doctor, hot on his heels. Frank hovered by the bathroom, pressing himself against the wall as though fearful of being asked to leave.

Running his eyes down the charts, the doctor questioned Lola with short, staccato sentences, before inspecting her entry point and explaining the bruising around the area where they inserted the stent would fade in a few days. Then he gave her a swift smile and delivered a volley of instructions to the nurse before striding out again.

Ryan passed her a water bottle, and she took a sip through the paper straw to moisten her throat. 'Have you spoken to Zoe?' she asked.

'Not yet. Too early. I'll send her a message after we've all had breakfast and ring later.' He grinned at Frank. 'There's a nice café downstairs, Dad. Not as good as Mum's, of course, but they do a good eggs benny.'

Frank nodded, returning to Lola's bedside and laying a hand gently on her arm. 'Will you be okay if I leave you for half an hour?'

With a soft smile, she nodded. 'I'll be fine. Enjoy your breakfast.'

As he left the room, her heart gave an involuntary skip of happiness. For more than fifty years, she and Frank had lived, loved, and worked together. Now their beloved son had returned to the fold and her cup was full. Her dodgy heart had given them all a fright, but she gave thanks for modern medicine—and the practical, rapid action of both Emma and Zoe.

I'll be home soon.

29

*V*oices, mingled with the smell of coffee, woke Zoe. She shot up in bed, confusion clouding her head for a few moments. Then, remembering where she was, she slipped out of bed, quickly dressed, and walked along the huge hallway to the living room.

'Morning.' Kirk's wide grin greeted her. In the farm kitchen beyond the lounge and dining areas, he held up a mug in one hand while milk frothed noisily in the machine. 'Coffee?'

'Thanks. Sounds great.'

Ginny shuffled along the polished boards in soft-soled slippers, coming up behind Zoe and placing a kiss on her cheek. 'Merry Christmas, Zoe.'

Zoe turned abruptly, her gaze resting on the huge, decorated Christmas tree in the corner of the room, and her turquoise eyes widened. 'I forgot! Merry Christmas.'

'Have you heard how Lola is this morning?' Ginny asked.

'No. Not yet. I expect Dad will ring or message soon, but things sounded good last night.'

Ginny smiled then, pursing her lips, she looked at Kirk. 'It will not be quite the day we had planned.'

'What. Another change?' Kirk continued with his coffee-making until three steaming mugs stood in a row on the bench.

'Yes. Briony and Alex can't make it.' Ginny huffed a disappointed sigh and turned to Zoe. 'They're working in a high-end tourist resort on the Gold Coast now and had negotiated two days off over Christmas when they took the job on a few weeks ago. Apparently, the new shift manager forgot and rostered them both on for today and tomorrow. They only found out last night when one of their colleagues said something about "hoping they didn't have to deal with demanding holiday customers". Briony's furious. Because their shifts didn't finish until ten last night, they even had the car packed ready for an early start today. Now they've got to be back at work this morning.'

'Oh.' Zoe thought about the previous evening when she had helped Ginny unpack the esky and tidy the kitchen. It had been hard squeezing the leftover grated cheese in the fridge as a huge turkey commanded an entire shelf while an assortment of desserts surrounded other items. 'If it's going to be a small crowd, I guess we need to be hungry.'

Ginny chuckled with her. 'Yes. Most things will keep for a couple of days, anyway—and if I cook it all this morning, I won't have to do much for a while.'

'How many have we got for lunch now, love?' Kirk asked.

'Us, Claire and Rhys, and Sarah and Andrew.'

Zoe's heart leapt. Andrew. She hadn't seen him since the hay-making weekend, and it would be good to talk again. Although she would miss having her father and grandparents with them, seven people were still a sizeable crowd. Hoping the heat that was creeping up her neck didn't give her thoughts away, she clasped the mug and turned toward the veranda while she took a sip.

The neatly mown lawn was strewn with leaves and twigs after the night's blustery winds. A tiny bird nest lay on the grass near the hedge and Zoe narrowed her eyes, pointing as Ginny appeared at her shoulder. 'I hope the little birds have flown?'

'They would have. By now, they're probably helping themselves to the insects in that garden.' Ginny nodded toward a huge central garden bed where rows of flowers surrounded a circle of multicoloured roses.

'You must be disappointed about today,' Zoe said.

'You mean about Briony and Alex not making it? And your family, of course.'

'Yes.'

Ginny drew a deep breath. 'Not anymore. There was a time when I got upset when plans changed, especially if I'd spent days preparing. But now, I know how little control we actually have over these things, and I take everything as it comes.' She put an arm around Zoe's shoulders and squeezed. 'Anyway, in some ways it's good that Lola's in hospital and not here. If she were—here, I mean—and that heart condition worsened, the outcome could have been much worse.'

Zoe grimaced. She hadn't thought of that. Her phone pinged, and she reached into her back pocket to extract it. 'It's from Dad.' She scanned it briefly before adding, 'I'll read it out.'

'*Merry Christmas! I'm so sorry I can't be with you today. All good here. Mum's looking much brighter, and the doctor has already been to see her. They're moving her from intensive care to a private room later today. I'll hang around until this afternoon and make sure Dad has everything he needs in the motel. They won't discharge her on a public holiday, but it looks as though she'll be coming home the day after Boxing Day. He reckons he doesn't need the car. The motel is only two hundred metres from the hospital. Will keep you posted. Love, Dad.*'

Zoe looked up, smiling. 'Isn't that good? Imagine

that? In a helicopter yesterday and seriously ill. Then in two days' time she'll be back home again.'

Kirk shot her a wry grin. 'Yeah. The doctor probably wants to spend his Christmas with family, too.'

'Come on, Zoe.' Ginny intervened. 'You feed Pixie while I cook breakfast. Claire will be here soon to collect you.'

'Okay. I'll just message Dad back.'

As she tapped the phone, a surge of excitement rose inside her, mixed with determination. Everything was going to be alright. She was a grown woman— well, almost. Growing up came with responsibilities and today she had plenty of them. It was time to step up.

30

*E*mma bit her lip as she loaded the bottles of soft drink and bag of cheeses into her car. Was it enough? Nothing was handmade or personal and this year her usual enthusiasm for a day with her noisy, encompassing Italian friends was lacking.

Inside the car boot, resting beside the esky, was a box containing two bottles of red wine and two of white. Maria was always insistent she bring nothing but herself, but Emma had never arrived at a friend's home empty-handed, and she wasn't about to start now, regardless of how tired she was.

The previous night's drive back to Featherwood Falls had seemed interminable. Ryan had been waiting anxiously for her, insisting she send a text, even if he slept through it, when she reached Warwick to let him know she only had an hour to drive before reaching home.

After a quick hug and cup of tea together, Ryan had left for Brisbane and Emma had given a jubilant Piccolo a quick run around the yard and a bone to chew on before she crawled into bed.

Now she wearily watched the power poles and paddocks fly past as she drove south-east toward Stanthorpe.

Half an hour later, she turned into the gravel driveway lined on either side with rows of perfectly spaced fruit trees. The sprawling timber home, dwarfed by the enormous packing shed behind it, was surrounded by freshly mown lawns and hydrangea-and-geranium-filled garden beds. Emma registered the new, net-covered plantations of apple trees and the second dwelling partially hidden by a hedge. She smiled. That must be the house Maria had spoken of for their eldest son, Tony, and his new wife, Francesca. For more than a year, they had lived with Maria and Joseph, along with their other five children, and now, with a young baby to care for, she imagined how delighted the young couple would be to have their own home.

Greeted with hugs and excited children, Emma did the rounds, introducing herself to friends and relations of Maria and Joseph's she had not met before, and being smothered in kisses by those she had.

For the first time since she had joined Maria's family for Christmas, Emma felt alone. Despite the encompassing and friendly conversations, the platters of food being foisted upon her, and the pile of delicious preserves and home-made soaps gifted to her, all she wanted to do was to scurry back to Featherwood Falls, crawl into bed, and wait for Ryan to return.

Somehow, she made it through until almost four o'clock, refusing glasses of wine and opting for lemonade instead to clear her head. Graciously, she thanked Maria for her hospitality, shared a million kisses once again with Maria's family, and retreated to her car.

As Featherwood Falls came into view half an hour later, her phone pinged and she pulled over, anxious to read Ryan's message.

Dad's settled in and all is well. Will have dinner with him then head home. See you about ten. He ended the message with a series of heart emojis, and Emma quickly returned the text, adding her own row of kisses.

She pulled back onto the road with a huge sigh of relief, her mood lifting as love filled her soul.

What a strange Christmas this has been. She reflected on the quiet, frugal years of celebration with her mother. Following Maureen's death, Christmas with Maria and her family had been a joy—a welcome diversion and coming together of all things right and holy.

Now, she was surprised she longed for something different. A Christmas at her cottage—perhaps on the veranda with Lola and Frank, Ryan, Zoe, and Piccolo. Her own little family squished happily together.

She shook herself and drove into the garage, grinning at the sound of Piccolo's welcoming yips.

It was time to press the reset button.

31

*Z*oe stood back and admired the veranda table. Long and narrow, it seated twelve comfortably, but today, the silver-and-white placemats complete with gleaming cutlery numbered seven. Sprigs of ivy, squat vases of colourful flowers, and shiny bon-bons wove their way down the centre, leaving just enough room for platters and bowls of food to be placed in the gaps.

She pressed her fingers together and grinned at Claire. 'It looks awesome.'

'Yeah. Not too bad.'

A cloud of dust signalled the arrival of a vehicle in the driveway. Zoe rubbed her palms down the sides of her cotton dress—the short, puffed-sleeved one in shades of turquoise that exactly matched her eyes. She and Lola had bought it on their shopping spree in Warwick, and now Zoe wished more than ever that her grandmother was here to see it on her again.

Car doors slammed, and Andrew bounded along the paved path, a box of brightly wrapped gifts in his arms and a short, plump woman with curly, light brown hair and a pleasant face following him.

'Merry Christmas.' He kissed Ginny on the cheek, shook Kirk's hand, and gathered Claire, and then Zoe, into quick hugs.

Zoe flushed and stepped back, embarrassment rendering her speechless.

'Where's Rhys?' he asked.

'He'll be here in a jiffy. Had to do a couple of hours' work this morning.'

'Goodo. Hey, Zoe. You haven't met my mother.' He turned to the woman handing a large bowl of salad to Ginny. 'Mum, this is Zoe. Zoe, meet Sarah.'

Sarah extended a hand, a warm smile on her perfectly made-up face. 'Hello, Zoe. It's lovely to meet you.'

Hesitantly, Zoe reached out, accepting Sarah's gentle finger squeeze with a smile. 'Um. Nice to meet you, too.'

Although Sarah and Andrew shared similar colouring, the likeness stopped there. Once again, Zoe glanced from Claire to Andrew, recognizing the familiar build, expressions, and easy, lithe gait. Her gaze moved beyond the veranda to the parked cars. No Donald?

'What's Donald doing today?' Kirk asked.

Zoe stared at him. Had he read her mind?

'Who knows,' Sarah said tartly. 'He lives in Brisbane most of the time these days and tells me as little as possible. When he comes home to check on the farm or criticise Andrew, he doesn't even speak to me—and to be honest, that's okay. He probably had a big night on the booze last night and hasn't even woken up yet.'

Ginny's eye roll suggested to Zoe this was not a surprise, while Claire's relieved smile indicated his absence was welcome.

Before they could say more, a police vehicle roared up the drive.

'Great. Rhys is here,' Ginny said, turning to Kirk. 'Would you open the wine please, darling? I'll get the fruit punch and check on the turkey.'

'I'm sorry to hear about Lola.' Andrew shot Zoe a sympathetic smile. 'Hospital's the best place for her today, I guess.'

Zoe swung her gaze around, momentarily puzzled. 'H-how did you know?'

Claire squeezed her shoulder. 'This is the country, Zoe. I imagine almost everyone in Featherwood Falls knows by now. The appearance of the ambulance would have started the word spreading and Janet wouldn't have held back. Don't worry though. People care about Lola and I've no doubt she'll be overrun with visitors—and you'll be swamped with casseroles and rice puddings when she gets home.'

Andrew pointed to Claire. 'And as for us knowing, blame her.'

'Well, your mum needed to know she didn't have to clean out the supermarket to feed us all today.'

'I hardly think making one salad would require "cleaning out the supermarket", Claire,' Sarah said with a chuckle, her amusement travelling to Zoe as she met the girl's questioning frown. 'I appreciated Claire's call last night. As you've probably heard, I rarely join in these family occasions, but that's not because I feel unwelcome. My marriage to Donald Shepherd has been a ... troubled one for many years, and to avoid family friction, I have felt it best to keep him away from here.'

'Not always successfully,' Claire quipped.

Rhys trod firmly up the steps and another round of handshakes and hugs ensued as Kirk and Ginny appeared with trays of drinks.

General chatter morphed to touching on specific details of the previous day's events and, by the time Kirk had carved the turkey and they'd filled the table with dishes of baked vegetables, salads and a platter of sliced ham, Zoe found all eyes on her.

'You poor thing,' Sarah said. 'Were you alone with Lola?'

Zoe drew breath and recounted the trauma, dismissing the waves of panic that threatened to re-emerge. 'Emma was fabulous. So calm and helpful. I'm pleased she and Dad have found each other again.'

Sarah's eyebrows rose, but she said nothing. Clearly that was a story for another time—and Zoe suspected questions would be asked of Ginny the minute Zoe was out of earshot.

A spread of chocolate mousse, fresh fruit salad, and a traditional Christmas pudding was devoured with lashings of cream and ice cream. The chatter had eased off and a peaceful contentment spread around the table.

The sun beat down with surprising ferocity after the previous night's cold change.

'Why don't you leave us to clear up here while you young ones go to the falls for a swim?' Ginny said.

'Good idea,' Sarah added. 'I'll give you and Kirk a hand, Ginny.'

Hoping her blush wasn't noticeable, Zoe attempted to stem the thrill that rapidly consumed her.

WITH TOWELS SLUNG over their shoulders and five kelpies milling around their feet, Rhys, Claire, Andrew, and Zoe trooped along the track and over the hill before descending twenty minutes later to a clump of native rainforest. As the sound of rushing water drew near, Zoe narrowed her eyes, gobsmacked at what she could only describe as the most beautiful pond she'd ever seen.

Claire led them through low shrubs before reaching a shelf of rocks edging the pool that nestled at the foot of an exquisite waterfall. Mesmerised, Zoe paused as water tinkled over multiple levels of boulders and tiny ponds before falling into the much larger pool in front of them.

A series of flat slabs of granite pressed into the ground on either side with ferns of every shape and shade of green pushing their way through the gaps, as though seeking maximum moisture while their roots remained warmly encased by rock.

'Wow. That's so cool.' Zoe released a long breath of admiration.

'Yeah. It is cool,' Andrew laughed. 'In more ways than one.' He kicked off a shoe and dipped his foot in the water. 'It's freezing.'

One by one, they stripped down to their swimmers and slid cautiously into the water.

Self-conscious in her maroon, school one-piece suit—the only one she owned—Zoe kept her towel around her until the very last moment, and tried not to gasp as her skin touched the icy liquid. Surprised to feel it was shallower than she had expected, she threw her towel onto a sun-soaked rock and struck out across the pool to where Claire lounged, her back pressed against the opposite bank.

'What a beautiful place. You must have had a lot of fun growing up,' she said to Claire.

'We did. Andrew too. My father did most of the work. It was just a stream years ago, but one summer holiday when I was quite small, Dad widened this area and turned it in to a place we could all enjoy. Over the years, we've added more rocks around the edges and on hot days I bring the dogs here for a swim too.'

Rhys drifted toward the girls, his face to the sky and with shoulder muscles rippling as he leisurely stroked upward and back until his head bumped Claire's stomach and he stood up without apology.

'I'm the buffer now, I see,' Claire laughed. 'This is not an Olympic swimming pool.'

'Yeah, well. Better than knocking my head against the rocks.' Rhys slid his arm around his wife, and they pressed their bodies together, kissing and seemingly oblivious to any other presence.

A loud splash brought a shriek from Zoe as water cascaded over the three of them.

Andrew's head popped out of the pool, a grin spreading across his face. 'Just reminding you we're here too.' His smile focused on Zoe. 'Take no notice of the lovebirds. They've only been married a few weeks, so the honeymoon isn't over yet.'

Zoe giggled, grateful for the way he eased her embarrassment. She shivered, and a frown of concern crossed his face.

'Don't let yourself get cold. Last thing Lola needs when she gets home is a granddaughter coming down with something.'

Zoe nodded, looking down at her thin, goose-bumped arms. 'I'll sit on the rocks for a while and warm up.' Then she stroked slowly across the pool again, hauled herself out, and reached for her towel before sitting companionably between Drum and Banjo.

The afternoon drifted on. Clouds scudded across the sky, and by three o'clock, all four of them decided it was time to head back to the homestead.

As they walked, Andrew's easy conversation and caring, considerate questions broadened, and Zoe relaxed completely, sharing more of her past than she had ever told anyone, including Amy and Natalia.

Again, while still missing her friends and with some remaining homesickness for her lost city life, Zoe was surprised how much she was enjoying living in Featherwood Falls—especially with the amount of love and attention that now enveloped her. Despite the trauma and anxiety of Lola being whipped off to hospital, today had been the best Christmas in years. In two days' time, her grandmother would be home again and they would open their gifts, hug each other, and have another special dinner.

Until then, she would stay here with Ginny and Kirk, care for Pixie, and feed the other animals twice a day—and look forward to the Brown family being together again.

32

*C*rouched in a squat, Zoe unpacked the carton of cereal and was neatly arranging the boxes on the shelf when the doorbell rang. She glanced over her shoulder toward the counter, checking Janet hadn't nipped out the back. Good. She was facing the door, and Zoe wouldn't have to interrupt what she was doing to serve the customer.

'Good morning,' Janet said brightly. 'How can I help?'

'Yeah, gidday.' The gravelly voice paused for a second. 'I'll have a flat white and a copy of *The Land* thanks.' The man cleared his throat before adding, 'Like to keep abreast of what's happening. You know how it is when you're a landowner.'

Zoe froze, horror clawing at her throat. That voice. She couldn't be certain though—not yet. Crouching lower, she barely breathed, and the ticking minutes seemed to go on forever as the coffee machine hissed. Eventually, the card reader beeped, and the man clumped his way outside.

Turning her head and peering through the curtain of hair that veiled her face, Zoe glimpsed him getting into a burgundy-coloured four-wheel drive. He turned and glanced her way before the vehicle moved. Uncertainty bit deep. What was he doing in Featherwood Falls? Her view of the familiar bulky frame had been clear. There was no doubt in her mind that this man was dangerous.

A lump of terror filled the back of her throat. With shaking hands, she quickly emptied the box, rose silently to her feet, and fled through the kitchen, ignoring Janet's puzzled expression.

Pressing her back against the shed door, she forced deep breaths in and out of her lungs while edging toward the corner of the building and sliding her gaze up and down the main road. The rumble of a diesel engine faded into the distance. For long minutes, she didn't dare move for fear of its return.

Blood pounded in her ears as a million thoughts tumbled in her head. Would he know her? The overheard park conversation and her mother's death rolled around her head in a tangled mess. Adrian clearly had links to this man—so what did that mean for her? Did Adrian think she had told the police about his drug dealing, and that there was a link there somewhere? Was Adrian somewhere here in Featherwood Falls too?

She had to get away.

With a quick glance around, she welcomed the silent emptiness of the town. It would be another four hours before Ginny and Frank returned, bringing Lola home from hospital. Her father and Emma had gone goodness knows where for a belated Christmas picnic. So, it was only her and Janet minding the shop.

Panic took flight inside her as possibilities multiplied. She couldn't risk hanging around. He might return to seek her out—and then she'd be dead meat for certain.

With her head bowed, she darted across the back paddock, through Frank's brand-new gate, and into the bush. Following the trail through long grass frequented by the kangaroos, she broke into a jog, her breath cracking with sobs. Barely aware of her surroundings, she turned at the fork, taking the less-travelled track toward the hills. Leaves brushed her face, and branches snagged her leggings as she ran. Her chest burned with exertion, and she slowed to a brisk walk as she reached the lookout where she had stopped with Emma and Piccolo weeks earlier.

In the distance, a shimmer of the midday sun flickered on the iron roof of the timber-cutter's hut.

Relief mixed with apprehension churned in her gut. It was tumble-down, and Emma had suggested it was spooky, but it was shelter. Somewhere to hide. Beyond getting caught by that loathsome man, she hadn't given her situation another thought.

SHE BROKE INTO A TROT AGAIN, now in unfamiliar territory. The track faded in and out of young saplings and branches tossed to the ground like matchsticks following a storm, forcing her to slow. Fresh growth surrounded her, whipping at her legs and grasping strands of hair as she pushed forward. Reaching a rocky outcrop where only grass trees and clumps of tussock stood, she stopped and let her eyes wander. Beyond the scattering of rocks and boulders, the timber walls of the hut stood solid and forlorn. She drew closer, absorbing the spiderweb-covered windows with their tinge of green mildew, the broken plank on the veranda, and the loose, flapping sheet of iron on the roof. An icy shiver ran down her spine.

Up close, it didn't look as cute as it had from a distance. Her shoulders sagged. She had no choice. It was this—or return to the village, pretend nothing had happened, and be paralysed with fear.

Taking careful, delicate steps over the creaking veranda, she pushed open the door, swollen with age and damp. It slid, rasping against the warped floorboards. A fierce fluttering drew a shriek from her as a flock of birds took flight, crashing their way around the cabin before fleeing through the open door.

'Oh, God. I can't do this.' Stepping back, she stared at the way she had come. The distant hum of a tractor filtered up through the valley, mixing with the sounds of bird calls. She held a hand against her chest as though commanding her thumping heart to settle. In that moment, her inquisitive nature overruled her fear and she turned to peer into the dark haven that lay before her.

Sucking in a deep breath, she stepped inside, pausing while her eyes adjusted to the poor light.

On one side of the square, one-room cabin, an ancient, single-width bed pressed against the wall, its mattress completely covered with a canvas tarpaulin. She cautiously lifted one corner of the covering, then drew it right back until it exposed a surprisingly clean blanket beneath wearing no signs of mouse dirt or damage. Her mouth quirked. Is this where her father and Emma had hung out years earlier? Surprised that other teenagers hadn't followed suit, she swung her gaze to the other side of the room. A metal cupboard with a thick gauze door hung on the wall above a tiny table and two handmade chairs. One of these was capsized on the floor, so she picked it up and brushed the dust off her hands, rubbing them down her shirt.

She prized the door of the cupboard open, breaking a nail with the exertion. Inside, a row of four tin canisters filled the bottom shelf. Above them sat a box of matches, a packet of candles, two chipped china mugs and, standing on their edge with backs against the rear of the cabinet, three enamel plates.

Picking off the remnants of her broken nail, she swung her gaze to the brick fireplace on the back wall, its voluminous chimney dominating the room. A blackened kettle—the type you saw hanging above a campfire—rested on the wide, stone hearth alongside an elaborately constructed poker and a worn, straw broom.

Intrigued now, Zoe returned to the cabinet, removed the lids of the canisters one by one, and inspected their contents.

Screwing up her nose, she held the first container at a distance before taking a second peep. A solid brown cake of what may have once been instant coffee was now covered in furry mildew. She found more matches in one, a white substance in another that could have been milk powder or sugar—she wasn't sure which—and loose tea leaves that were also wearing a coating of mildew in the final tin.

Returning to the rickety veranda, she squatted on the edge of a board that looked relatively whole and stared back down the valley. Light slanted through the trees below, painting stripes on the boulders strewn across the tawny-coloured grass.

With her arms wrapped around her legs and her

knees pulled up to her chin, Zoe wasn't sure how long she sat there. Her pulse had slowed but fear still clogged her veins and her ability to think straight. The sun crept behind charcoal-tinted ranges on the opposite side of the valley and an icy breeze filtered up the rise, rustling leaves and aiding a hawk's leisurely cruise as it rode the thermals.

Hunger gnawed at her stomach, and she shivered, rubbing her upper arms before clutching her folded legs tighter to instil some warmth into her bloodstream.

An image of her mother floated above her, and she leaned her forehead on her knees.

Oh, Mum. Why? Why did you have to leave? Why couldn't you see what was happening?

Tears pricked the backs of her eyes as terror and self-pity mingled. She had shed a few tears following Catherine's death, but until today's scare, her anger and disappointment had prevented more. Now, as the hopelessness consumed her once again, she let the tears flow.

Loud sobbing filled her ears, and she rocked back and forth, her weeping soaking the front of her shirt. Long minutes later, she lifted her head, peering through misty, swollen eyes, surprised the sun had gone and the forest birds had quietened.

Retreating to the cabin, she hauled the tarpaulin off the bed, stripped the blanket, and took it outside to shake. Sneezing as dust flew, she examined it. There were a few holes in one corner, as though it had caught on something—or some tiny creature had chewed it. She shuddered again, flicking it in the cooling night air. Exhausted and cold, she folded it in half, wrapped it around herself, and lay on the bed. Something skittered across the roof. A gust of wind caught the edge of loose iron, bashing it noisily. Covering her head with the blanket, Zoe plugged her ears with her fingers, curled into a ball, and fell into a troubled sleep.

33

*E*mma and Ryan reached the car as the afternoon sun faded to the west, shedding their backpacks into the boot before sliding onto the front seats.

'Thanks for a lovely day,' Emma breathed.

Ryan stroked her hair, tucking loose strands behind her ear. 'Thanks for making it so perfect. It's been decades since I've been here and even though the crowds were ten times bigger than when we were teenagers, I enjoyed it just as much.'

'Me too. I'd heard they'd done a lot of improvements in Girraween but didn't realise how popular those improvements have made it. Imagine trying to get a campsite here now. These poor people must have had to book a year ago.'

'Yeah. And I'm not sure I'd want my neighbours so close—especially with only a thin piece of canvas or nylon between us.' He laughed then, and their eyes met with a knowing sparkle. 'Let's get home. Ginny will be back with Mum and Dad soon and Zoe will appreciate a hand to feed up.'

'Okay. I'm looking forward to a turkey and roast vegetable dinner. Maria's a fabulous cook and I enjoy Italian cuisine, but you can't beat the traditional dinners we grew up with.'

He covered her hand with his, swung the wheel with the other, and drove slowly out of the park.

'WHAT DO YOU MEAN, she's gone?' Ryan asked, his voice louder than she'd ever heard it.

Janet held her hands upturned, a concerned frown on her forehead. 'She's not here. I've looked everywhere. Even rang Claire. She said she's probably gone for a walk and if she's not back by dark, she'd come and help me look for her. Zoe didn't say anything to me. One minute she was packing shelves and the next, she was gone. But now you're home—do you want me to lock up?'

Ryan nodded. 'Yes, please.' He turned to Emma, his face creased with concern. 'Would she have gone to your place?'

'Possibly. I'll nip home and check.'

Emma paused as he continued, speaking in a rapid, almost panicked tone. 'Janet, do you know if the animals have been fed?'

'I doubt it. Zoe's been gone since early afternoon. Every time the doorbell rang, I thought it would be her —but it wasn't. I asked the late-afternoon local customers if anyone had seen her, but they said no. The little kangaroo was calling earlier, so I nipped in and gave her a bottle of milk. Luckily, Lola had shown me where all that stuff is kept in case I ever needed to give her a hand.'

'Thank you.' He lowered his voice, as if fighting to stay calm. 'I appreciate your help. I'll feed the animals now while you lock up. Let me know if you see her and I'll do the same when she turns up.'

As the woman disappeared into the post office, Emma and Ryan faced each other.

At the unease reflected in Ryan's eyes, Emma squeezed his hand. 'I'll ring you as soon as I've checked my place.'

She fled out the front door, her shoulder-bag flapping against her hip as she ran.

A welcome yip sounded from Piccolo's pen as she opened the front gate. Her frown deepened. If Piccolo was still locked up, it was unlikely Zoe would be around, even though she and Emma had agreed she could unlock the house and play the piano during the day if she wanted to. But today was different. Lola was in hospital and Zoe was the one who had assured both Emma and her father that she was reliable and would help Janet while they were away.

Struggling against all reasoning, Emma unlocked the door, her heart giving an involuntary skip of terror as the empty silence greeted her.

'Zoe! Are you here?'

Nothing.

She darted in and out of each room before leaping down the back stairs and letting Piccolo out of her pen. The dog dashed around her in excited circles as Emma's heart sank.

Pressing Ryan's number, she held the phone against her ear.

'Is she there?' Ryan's gravel-rough voice deepened, laced with the hint of hope.

'No. And Piccolo is crazy with energy, so she obviously hasn't been here all day. If she had, Piccolo would be more settled. I think we should ring Rhys.'

Seconds of silence greeted her before he spoke. 'Okay. I'll finish here then meet you at the police station.'

CLAIRE ENTERED the reception area via the passage adjoining the police house with the station at the same time Emma stepped through the door.

'Hi, Emma.' Claire's bright smile faded as Emma leaned on the counter, panting with exertion.

Before either could say another word, the thumping of heavy footsteps coming up the path sounded, and Ryan burst through the entrance.

'What's the problem?' Claire asked.

'Zoe's missing. Is Rhys here?' Ryan peered over the counter, his gaze roving the room as if expecting Rhys to pop out of a cupboard.

'He's out the back. I'll get him.' Claire strode down the corridor as Emma gripped Ryan's arm.

'Let's stay calm. Zoe's a teenager and despite her maturity, she's probably just forgotten she promised to help Janet. Maybe she was tired and fell asleep in her room. Did anyone check the house thoroughly?'

'I did. After you left. She's been watching that series called *Stranger Things* on her laptop, so I thought she might be catching up on an episode or something,' he finished lamely as they stared at each other and simultaneously shook their heads. 'No. Of course not. She wouldn't do that when she had work to do,' he sighed.

Rhys and Claire returned at that moment, and Rhys beckoned them into the office. 'Sit down and let's run through the possibilities.' His friendly ease held a professional edge as he grabbed a pen and paper.

After repeating the conversation they had shared with Janet less than half an hour earlier, both Emma and Ryan stared at Rhys while he jotted down key elements.

Rhys glanced at Claire. 'She's not up at the farm, is she?'

Claire frowned, shaking her head. 'No. Mum's gone to Brisbane to collect Lola and Frank, and Kirk and I spent most of the day drenching lambs. Anyway, we knew she and Janet were looking after the shop today. We talked about it on Christmas day.'

He chewed the side of his lip and gave a nod. 'Right. First thing is to ring Janet and see if she can remember anything that may have happened in the shop preceding Zoe disappearing.' Rhys pressed his lips together as he picked up the landline receiver. 'Do you have her number?'

Turning his palm over, Ryan glanced down and recited the numbers scrawled across his hand.

Emma raised her eyebrows, and he shot her a wry grin. 'Thought he'd want to talk to her, so I grabbed her number before she went home.'

'Hi, Janet.' Rhys pressed the speaker button on the handpiece and lay it on the desk. 'Rhys here. I've got Emma and Ryan with me. They're worried about Zoe, and we wondered if you could help.'

A woman's throat-clearing rattle echoed through the line. 'Sure. As I said to Ryan, she just disappeared. One minute she was unpacking boxes and tidying shelves and the next, she was gone.'

'Okay. Did you see her leave?'

'Yes. She rushed past me while I was in the kitchen. Never came back. I thought perhaps she'd suddenly remembered to feed the little kangaroo or something, but that was not it. The joey started calling a couple of hours later and I had to go into the house to feed it.'

'And when you were in the house, there was no sign of Zoe?'

'No. Nothing. Apart from the joey yelling for food, the house was quiet.'

'Okay. Do you remember what you were doing when she left?'

'In the shop, you mean?'

'Yes. Were you helping her pack shelves—or serving a customer?'

'Neither—' She stopped abruptly, and Rhys glanced up, shooting the others a troubled gaze before she continued. 'Oh, hang on. There was a customer just before she left. A fella came in for a copy of *The Land* and a coffee. Flat white, it was. That's right. He'd just left, and I was wiping the coffee machine down when Zoe dashed into the house.'

Rhys's shoulders softened. 'Okay. Had Zoe shown

any interest in the customer? Offered to serve him before you, for example?'

'No. Nothing like that. As I said, she was emptying a box of cereal packets. I think she would have been kneeling on the floor or bending over behind the shelving unit. They probably didn't even see each other. She knew I was there and ...' She paused as though dredging her memory for more. 'Yeah, I looked up when the doorbell chimed as the fella walked in, so I said, "Gidday" and then asked if I could help him. Zoe just kept doing her work, I think. I didn't hear her.'

'You didn't hear her?'

'That's right. You know—when you're unpacking a box, you usually make a bit of a racket. Shifting stuff around on the shelves. I do, anyway.'

'So, Zoe was silent.'

'Well. I couldn't be sure. But she certainly wasn't noisy.' She chuckled. 'As a matter of fact, she's the opposite of Lola. We always know where she is, but Zoe is quiet. I often get a fright when she suddenly appears beside me.'

Claire rolled her eyes at the others as Rhys persevered. 'Can you remember what this man looked like?'

'A big fella. Not particularly tall but with a big belly and one of those red, puffy faces that looks like he's been in the sun too long or has a good relationship with the bottle.'

'So, you didn't know him?'

'No. His car was parked right outside the front door though—blocking anyone else if they'd wanted to buy fuel.'

Rhys raised his eyes and gave the others a tiny nod. 'Okay. Do you remember what sort of vehicle it was?'

'Umm. A dark red sort of colour. Maroon, I suppose you'd call it. A biggish four-wheel drive. Maybe a LandCruiser or one of those Isuzu wagons. Sorry. I'm not very good with vehicles.'

'That's okay, Janet. Except for this customer, is there anything else you can think of that may have given Zoe a fright?'

'I don't think so. We keep the shop clean, so there're no spiders or stuff like that.'

'Thank you. You've been extremely helpful.'

'You're welcome. She's a nice kid.' She hesitated for a second. 'Would you let me know when you find her, please?'

Rhys breathed out a sigh. 'Yes, of course, Janet. We'll do that.'

He replaced the handpiece in its cradle and rubbed a hand through his short, brown hair.

'Well. It looks like we'd better put the call out. Something or someone has caused Zoe to behave abnormally—for her, anyway. This is a small town, but it's surrounded by bush and she could be anywhere.' He narrowed his eyes while the others stared at him in silence. 'She's only been here a few weeks, so wouldn't know her way around the hills like the rest of us do. I'll call Damian and get him to rally the emergency-service volunteers.'

For a few seconds, silence embraced them all. Then, as Emma gazed into Ryan's stricken face, fear tore at her soul.

34

*W*earing a head torch and a warm jacket, Emma gripped Piccolo's leash tightly as the dog pulled against her hold.

'No, Piccolo. We're going this way.'

The crowd of volunteers had grown, and they'd divided into four groups to search each corner of the valley before splitting into pairs. Then, methodically combing the network of narrow roads and tracks that encircled Featherwood Falls, they communicated by two-way handpieces and recognised one another by the bright luminous stripes that criss-crossed orange overalls. Pinpricks of light bobbed their way along trails while powerful search beams roved the hillsides and voices called.

Emma and Piccolo trotted after Ryan, inspecting patches of flattened grass, kangaroo tracks, and every

nook and cranny offering shelter for a slight, frightened girl.

Although only a little after seven, a clouded, black
sky hung above them and a strong breeze wailed up
the valley. Emma leaned, panting, against Ryan as he
paused for breath.

Together with Claire, Rhys, and a handful of locals,
they had elected to comb the familiar eastern tracks of
the valley while Kirk led a team into the western gran-
ite-covered hills pocked with trickling springs and
unexpected crevices. To the south, Damian
commanded another team of a dozen men and
women, checking every patch of bushland and skeletal
remnants of recently burned-out forest that had been
devastated by fires that had raged only months earlier.

With every step, Emma sensed Ryan's increasing
despair. Two months earlier, he hadn't even known he
had a daughter. Now he and Zoe had found each other
and bonded in what she could only describe as an
incredible stroke of both good luck and good fortune.
Respect and love for one another were palpable, the
invisible blood ties stronger than either could have
imagined.

She swallowed a choking sob as Piccolo jerked her
arm once more.

Please, God, let her be safe. Let us find her.

'Piccolo. Stop it!' she snapped, shoving a thrashing
tree branch from her face.

'She wants to go up that track, Emma.' Ryan studied the dog's pricked ears and keen, twitching nose. 'Have you ever walked her up there?'

He didn't say it, but the words were on the tip of his tongue. *Our track.*

'No, never. Zoe and I have been up here lots of times, but we always turn back at the lookout.'

He shrugged. 'Well, the way she's hauling you along, she looks like she wants to go that way now.'

Emma froze. 'Ryan!'

He halted immediately, reaching to grasp a tree as though her call had been a warning of some sort.

'The hut.'

The beam of her head torch shone in his eyes, and he raised his arm against his face.

'Sorry,' she said, switching the light from spotlight power to the dull red of the night-light.

'Do you mean the old timber-cutter's cabin?' he asked.

'Yes. When she saw it for the first time, she wanted to have a closer look.' She dropped her gaze and shuffled a foot in the dead leaves. 'I didn't want anyone to see our special place. Hardly anyone ever comes this way and I still think of it as being ours.'

He stepped toward her and gathered her against his chest. 'Oh, Emma. Those memories will always be with us.' His voice softened as his cheek brushed hers. 'Even if it's full of possums and stinks of bat poo.'

'Yuk!' She reeled, meeting his gaze as his face grew solemn. 'Do you really think she might go there?'

'There's only one way to find out.'

He spun on his heel, reached out to take the leash from Emma, and strode after the little dog.

ZOE WASN'T sure what woke her. The tin flapped above her, and something scurried across the floor. She hugged the blanket around herself, sneezing as the dust and mould particles invaded her nose.

Hunger pangs gripped her stomach. Terrified, the tears now spent and dry, she leaned against the wall, her arms wrapped tightly around bent knees.

Vivid memories of life before drugs—LBD, she privately called it—filled her mind. Visits to the botanic gardens during the cooler months. Swimming and skylarking at the South Bank pools with her mother, quiet visits to the library where they chose books together and poured through the shelf of jigsaw puzzles, searching for one they hadn't already done. Fish and chips on the riverbank.

Oh, Mum. Why did you let him take over our lives?

The sound of the man's voice echoed in her ears. The threatening words in the park had confused her. What had he meant? Adrian knew him—and her. Although he had often told her to "piss off" and she'd willingly run to Mrs Worth's unit for the rest of the night, there was something about the fat man that Adrian was frightened of. He had referred to him as "Boss". What did that mean?

She bit back the nightmarish event, dragging her thoughts to her grandmother. An ache formed in the bottom of her stomach that had nothing to do with hunger. Zoe loved Lola. From the day they had met, she had been a solid, reliable warmth in Zoe's short life. Her vivacious, friendly kindness was neither gushy nor reserved. Lola was exactly what Zoe had imagined a grandmother would be like—and both Frank and Ryan were pretty cool, too.

'And now I've let you all down,' she mumbled. 'You trusted me to help Janet and feed the animals. That was all. Easy. And I blew it.' Tears threatened again, surprising her. She didn't think she had a drop of moisture left in her body to spill.

Wracked with torment, she continued rocking back and forth as the wind howled outside and the iron sheeting banged.

It took another ten minutes before she decided. Running from a voice that she may or may not have imagined was "the man" was both immature and stupid. Her dad and Emma would be home by now and would be worried. She hadn't fed Pixie and she would be hopping around the house, peeing in places she wasn't supposed to be. What if Lola had tried to ring her? She glanced at her phone. No bars and no messages.

After shaking the blanket from her shoulders, she lay it over the bed again, tucking the sides under the mattress to prevent it from touching the floor, then she spread the tarpaulin over it, also ensuring it was securely fastened and covering every centimetre of the scratchy blanket.

As she tugged the door open, gritting her teeth as the swollen, ancient timber screeched against the floorboards, she noticed the wind had dropped.

A high-pitched bark sounded. Not the shriek of a fox or the howl of a dingo. This was the cry of a dog like Piccolo. A normal, kelpie-sounding bark.

Her heart leaped as a human call drifted up the valley. 'Zo-ee!'

Ryan? Was that her father? She paused, teetering on the edge of the veranda, straining to hear the call again.

Away to her right, pinpricks of light emerged from the bush. She gulped, her body shaking uncontrollably, uncertain. What if it was "the man"? Where else could she hide?

'Zo-ee! Can you hear me!' The call came again, and her heart leapt with relieved anticipation.

'I'm here,' she croaked. Then, rushing toward the lights, she called louder, 'Dad! I'm here.'

Tripping over rocks and sidestepping grass trees

and clumps of tussock, she ran as fast as she could toward them.

'Dad,' she breathed as he reached her and snatched her up as though she were a toddler while Piccolo jumped around them and spun in delighted circles.

'Thank God you're okay, Zoe.' He set her down, blinding her with his headlamp as he studied her. '*Are* you okay?'

She held her arm over her eyes and nodded, unable to speak.

'You darling girl. You gave us an awful fright.' Emma's arms wrapped around her, and Zoe leaned into the scent of the Daisy perfume she had become so familiar with.

Ryan shed his jacket before laying it around Zoe's shoulders. 'Come on. Let's get you home now and we can talk later.'

With a contented Piccolo leading the group while rigidly attached to Ryan, Zoe in the middle, and Emma bringing up the rear, they began the long tramp homeward.

35

*S*lumped in the passenger seat with exhaustion, Lola brightened a little as they slowed in preparation for turning into their tiny side street, relieved to have finally reached home. It had been one of the longest days she remembered. The long and short of it was that together with waiting on the hospital pharmacy, navigating hospital parking, and the chaotic afternoon city traffic—not to mention the multi-vehicle accident on the freeway—they'd left Brisbane more than four hours later than they'd planned. Two hours into their journey home, they'd mutually agreed they couldn't go any farther without sustenance. And they'd stopped in Warwick and enjoyed a restorative pot of tea and a toasted sandwich.

So, instead of the expected three o'clock arrival in

Featherwood Falls, it was almost nine by the time they approached the village.

'Oh look! There's a crowd of people outside the police station and an awful lot of cars,' Ginny said, worry creeping into her voice. 'Something must have happened.'

Lola leaned forward, her fatigue mildly reduced by interest. Under the beam of vehicle lights, Rhys appeared to be talking to a group of overalls-clad men and women, the iridescent stripes across their clothing shining white.

Ginny parked at the gate, and Frank removed the bags from the boot while she helped Lola out of the vehicle.

'I wonder what's going on?' Lola said, straightening while her hand rested on the fence.

Except for the drinks fridge, where bright LED bulbs highlighted colourful rows of cans and bottles, the shop was in darkness. In contrast, light spilled from every window of the house.

The back door banged, and Ryan strode toward them, a welcome smile lighting up his face. 'Hi, Mum.' He wrapped Lola in a gentle hug and stepped back. 'You're looking better than you did a couple of days ago.'

She chuckled. 'I feel a lot better, too.' Peering around him, her brow furrowed. 'Those people are our

SES group, aren't they? Is there another bushfire somewhere?'

Hooking his arm into hers, he led her down the path. 'Let's get you and Dad inside. Then I'll fill you in.'

As she stepped through the doorway, Lola caught the silent, puzzled exchange between Frank and Ginny.

'Emma's got the kettle on—and we've heated some of that tomato soup you had in the freezer.' Ryan spoke rapidly, and Lola shot him a narrow-eyed glance.

'Where's Zoe?'

'In the shower.'

'Oh.' Lola nodded, settled herself in an armchair, and waited while Ryan and Emma bustled about in the kitchen with Frank and Ginny, wearing quizzical expressions, half-heartedly offering to help.

With each of them sitting at the table with a bowl of soup and a cup of tea in front of them, Ryan opened his mouth as if to speak then shut it again as Zoe entered the room.

'Nan! You're home.' Zoe's voice wobbled as she rushed over to Lola and hugged her before turning and giving Frank a quick peck on the cheek.

Lola frowned, reaching out and squeezing her hand. 'Yes, love. We're all home and everything's going to be fine. They've put this stent thing in to solve the problem and I'll be right as rain in a few days. Just have to get my energy back.'

'Is anyone going to tell us what's going on?' Frank asked.

'I'm so sorry.' Tears trickled down Zoe's face. 'It's all my fault.'

Lola dropped her spoon and tomato soup splashed on the tablecloth. 'What's your fault?'

Emma interrupted, standing up and passing a tissue to Zoe. 'Claire got your message about the delay, Ginny. Thanks for letting us know.'

Lola's gaze swung to Ginny. Too tired to send a text at the time, she had asked Ginny to update the family for her but had assumed Ginny's message had been sent to Ryan, not Claire.

'Rhys will be here soon. He wants to talk to Zoe, but before he does that, he's thanking the crew for their help tonight and giving us some time to explain everything,' Emma continued.

'So will someone please get on with it and tell us what is happening?' Frank said, his voice rising with exasperation.

'Zoe went missing.'

All heads swivelled and everyone stared at Zoe as she sat, ashen-faced at the end of the table.

'I didn't go missing. At least, I didn't think I was missing. I ... I just ran to get away from that man and didn't stop to think how much everyone would worry about me.' Zoe's voice wavered again, fading to a whisper.

Ryan lay a reassuring hand on Zoe's shoulder. 'Apparently, a customer came into the shop while Zoe was packing shelves. Janet served him, but Zoe recognised his voice. We're not sure who it was—and Rhys wants to get to the bottom of this in case it's someone ... well, for lots of reasons. Anyway, Zoe thought the voice belonged to someone who had frightened her in Brisbane—someone linked to Catherine's drug dealer. So, she panicked and ran into the bush.'

'And I fell asleep, so I didn't realise everyone was looking for me.'

Lola's eyes widened. 'But where did you hide? And fall asleep?'

'Remember that old timber-cutter's hut at the top of the valley? Hasn't been lived in for decades,' Ryan said, hurrying on without waiting for Zoe to answer. 'She hid there.'

'Good grief.' Frank rubbed his chin, his kind eyes wide and shiny with amazement. 'That's a tough walk for a girl on her own. How did you know it was there?'

Zoe looked up at Emma. 'I saw it one day when Emma and I were taking Piccolo for a walk. We didn't go near it, and I didn't mean to end up there. It's just ...' she shook her head. 'I don't know why I went there.' She shuddered. 'I was so frightened. The hut was scary —and it stinks, but if the man in the shop is who I think he is, that is much more terrifying.'

Lola pushed her chair backwards and eased herself

around the table to wrap Zoe in her arms. 'It's okay, love. We're here now and you're safe.'

A knock sounded at the back door, and Ryan hurried to answer it. 'Hi. Come in.'

Footsteps sounded, and Ryan reappeared with Rhys and Claire behind him.

They filled the next few minutes with general conversation, delight to see Lola home again, and grateful acceptances of both tea and soup. So, it was after ten o'clock before they were all seated in the lounge. Squeezed between Zoe and Frank, Lola held hands with both, as if the contact provided the lifeline she so desperately craved.

'I know we're all tired, but I wanted to be sure Zoe was okay,' Rhys said.

He fixed a steady, solemn gaze on Zoe. 'I'd like to get a few details tomorrow—after you've had a good sleep. I think your grandmother will appreciate a decent night, too. So ... would you mind coming to see me at the station, Zoe?'

She shot a worried glance at Ryan.

He nodded, a reassuring smile touching his face. 'I'll come with you, Zoe.'

'So will I,' Emma added.

'Okay. What time?' Zoe asked quietly.

'About ten?'

Tentative relief relaxed her tight face, and she gave Rhys a brief nod.

'Okay.' He placed his empty mug on the coffee table and reached a hand toward Claire. 'We'll head home and leave you to get to bed.'

Before they left, Ginny, Rhys, and Claire took turns to hug Lola—Claire lingering and squeezing Lola's hands with hers. 'It's so good to see you feeling better, Lola—and to have you home again.'

While Ryan and Emma walked to the gate with their visitors, Lola rose to her feet, her heart filled with gratitude and concern. 'Come on, love. I think it's time you and I get to bed. It's been a long day.'

Zoe drew a deep breath and clung to Lola's arm as they ambled through the door toward the bedrooms. 'You're not wrong.'

36

*W*ith butterflies circling inside her stomach, Zoe walked along the pavement with Ryan on one side of her and Emma on the other. Although feeling like a small child, she drew comfort from their presence—providing an unspoken, deep reassurance that everything would be alright.

A strange man was sitting in the office with Rhys when they arrived, causing a wave of startled panic to wash over Zoe.

'Hi, guys.' Rhys leapt to his feet and came to greet them. 'This is James Avery, a friend and colleague who was passing through this morning and called in for coffee.'

They shook hands with the visitor and hovered awkwardly while waiting for instructions.

A knot formed in Zoe's stomach. Bending slightly,

she breathed deeply to erase it. Was this James guy going to hang around while Rhys questioned her?

As though reading her mind, Rhys said, 'Zoe, I know this is daunting, but I hope you don't mind if James sits in on our chat. He's a detective and has been working on a couple of Featherwood Falls issues for a while now.'

Zoe glanced at the older man again, noting the short, greying hair and kind face. His voice was gentle when he spoke.

'I'd like to hear more, if you don't mind, Zoe? We've got a couple of unsolved cases on the books, and it's always good to find out all we can. You never know, one of these days something will tip the balance and we'll be able to tie up those loose ends,' he said.

She shrugged. 'Okay.'

Rhys locked the door and switched the phone over before ushering them all into a side room. James disappeared for a few moments before returning with a jug of water and five glasses.

Then, with James and Rhys on one side of the table, Emma and Zoe opposite them, and Ryan seated at the end, Rhys pushed a button on the tape recorder beside him and began. 'I've had a chat with Janet, and we've established the customer who caused you concern came into the shop while you were packing shelves, meaning Janet served him. Would you please confirm he is the man you were afraid of? The one who requested a copy of *The Land* and a flat white coffee?'

She nodded.

'Please answer for the tape, Zoe.'

'Yes,' she said in a small voice, her hand creeping into Emma's lap to clasp hers.

'And do you remember where you heard the man's voice before?'

'Yes ...' She opened her mouth and then shut it again.

'It's okay, Zoe. Take your time.'

'I only heard him once. I saw him talking to Adrian in the park near our house.' She inhaled a shuddering sniff.

'Who is Adrian?'

'Mum's dealer. I didn't realise that was what he was to begin with. Thought he was some dero Mum must have been working with—or maybe picked up at a nightclub. Sometimes she went out with her work friends.' She shrugged. 'It was a few months before I realised that after every one of his visits to our house, Mum was superwoman for days. Then she'd gradually get more tired and sick until he visited again, and she'd be okay. I'm not stupid. I knew what she was doing, even though I always stayed in my room when he came.'

'I see.'

'And this man, the one in the park, what made you frightened of him?'

'I saw him grab Adrian and hold a knife against his throat. He was talking quietly but it's only a small park and I squashed myself into the hedge so they couldn't see me, but I heard them.'

Rhys raised his eyebrows. 'Can you remember exactly what was said?'

'I'll try. *Adrian said, "She's threatening to go to the cops. What should I do?" Then the big guy held up one of those little clip-seal bags of white powder and said, "This will solve the problem." Adrian said, "I'm not going to do that" or something like that. Then the big man said, "You're forgetting who is in charge here. Do as you're told or no one will find your body". Then Adrian apologised and told the big man to leave it with him.*'

'Is there anything else you remember?'

Zoe huffed. 'Mum had thrown Adrian out the time before—said she was going to go clean and didn't want him to come around again.' She fell silent, reflecting on her mother's pleading promises when, in a desperate attempt to change their lives, Zoe had threatened to tell the guidance officer at school that her mother was a drug addict in the hope Catherine would seek help. For a while, Zoe thought her threat had worked. Catherine had been subdued, loving, and hints of their earlier happiness had returned. But then she'd come home from work late, bringing a pile of files with her, and the following day, Adrian had appeared once again.

'Okay. So, tell me, Zoe. What made you feel unsafe?'

'I haven't told anyone about this because I was afraid of what Adrian and the fat man might do to Mum and me,' she finished tiredly. 'And I didn't tell the police when Mum died, but she told me that Adrian had been around that day while I was at school. Then Mum died that afternoon, and I was worried there was a connection and that they would come after me next if I said anything.'

Emma shivered, and a tight wave of concern passed between James and Rhys.

'Okay, Zoe. I understand. You suspect this "fat man" is at the top end of the drug hierarchy—at least in the suburb you lived in—and that he may think that, if you had to, you could identify him and potentially risk his business—and his freedom.'

'Exactly.'

'Could you describe these two men, Zoe?' Rhys asked.

She took a deep breath. 'Well, Adrian is around Dad's age, I think, but he is skinny and stinks.'

'What colour hair and skin?'

'Brown hair and really white skin, like he hardly ever goes outside.'

'And the fat man?'

'He is older, but not as old as Nan and Pop. Maybe in his fifties? He is taller than Adrian.' She paused and looked at Ryan. 'Not as tall as Dad, but maybe about Pop's height. He is really overweight, but he looks quite strong, like he works out or does something that builds muscles. His face is round and red, and his hair is kind of a light colour that's going grey. He was wearing a blue shirt in the shop, but I can't remember anything else.'

'You've done well, thank you. Did you ever hear Adrian mention a name that could belong to his ... colleague?'

'The only name he ever said was something like "Ducky" or maybe it was supposed to be "Dougie". It meant nothing to me, but I remember when I heard it, I laughed. It sounded too weird to be a man's name. Imagine a drug dealer called Ducky. Reminded me of Donald Duck.'

James shot Rhys a flinty gaze.

'Okay, is there anything else you'd like to tell us, Zoe?' Rhys finished.

'No, I don't think so. That's all I know.'

'Fine, thank you.' He reached over and pushed the stop button on the tape recorder.

After another brief, neighbourly chat, they said goodbye and strolled back to the shop in silence.

Zoe gave a bitter, half-hearted attempt at a laugh as they pushed the door open to be greeted by a smiling

Janet and the fragrance of fresh-brewed coffee. Hatred festered inside her as she pictured her mother's body and the men she blamed for her death. She turned to face Ryan with a terrified, wide-eyed gaze. 'I know I did the wrong thing by running off and I'm sorry I put everyone to so much trouble. But if the police find that horrible man, will I have to go to court? Or see him again?'

Ryan shook his head, resting a tender hand on her shoulder. 'I doubt it, Zoe. By sharing all you know with the police, you've done well. Now it's over to them and we can concentrate on doing things together—beginning with that Christmas dinner some of us missed.'

The weight that had kept her struggling to think straight, suddenly lifted.

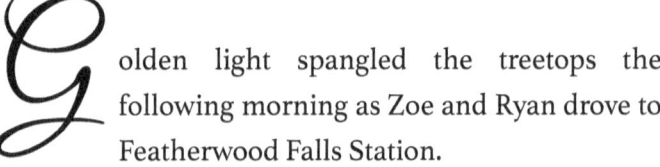 olden light spangled the treetops the following morning as Zoe and Ryan drove to Featherwood Falls Station.

Zoe had welcomed Claire's early-morning text, inviting her to help muster a flock of sheep that needed drenching. When she'd explained it would be an early start as, in summer, they liked to complete all animal work before the heat of the day seared them all, Zoe had jumped at the chance.

She had drifted into a deep, restorative sleep for hours the night before but had woken at first light and lain in bed listening to the sounds the new day. While her mind replayed the previous day's events, and guilt returned in waves, it surprised her how much her worries had eased. Sharing all she knew with Rhys and James had highlighted the stupidity of her running away, but it had also released the nagging apprehension that some of the knowledge she had shared with no-one until now, had been subconsciously gnawing away at her, threatening her chance of a peaceful future.

Seeing her grandmother home again, well and enthusiastic about returning to tend her business, had lifted Zoe's spirits in a way she had never imagined until now. Did this mean she was already becoming part of the Featherwood Falls community?

She chuckled aloud, and Ryan's head turned.

'What's funny?'

'Look at what I'm wearing.' She glanced down at her leggings and the worn, leather riding boots that Emma had loaned her, and rolled her eyes. 'If Amy and Natalia saw me, they'd reckon I'd turned from a city chick to jillaroo in a few short weeks.'

'And is that a bad thing?'

She screwed up her face. 'Dunno. I guess not. As long as I still get a good education and can go to uni, I suppose living in the country is okay—for now.'

He grunted a laugh. 'We'll get onto that in a couple of weeks.'

For the last few minutes of their drive, they sat in silence.

Claire was waiting at the gate when they arrived— the dogs milling around her feet and the two horses saddled ready.

Zoe walked over and patted Tango's neck, and Claire handed Zoe a helmet. 'Here you go.' Craning her neck at the car, she added, 'No Lola?'

Zoe shook her head. 'No, she's having a slow start. Frank's in the shop and said when Janet arrives, he will leave her to it and bring Nan here for a cuppa. He reckons that's the only way he's going to be able to keep her quiet for a couple of days.'

'Are you right now, Zoe?' Ryan called. 'I'll nip back and give Dad a hand.'

'Yeah. See you later. I'll come home with Nan and Pop.'

They waved goodbye before Zoe fastened her helmet and mounted Tango. The change of scenery, the exhilaration of riding, and Claire's quiet, capable company pushed all thoughts of the previous two days to the back of Zoe's mind.

STANDING in her stirrups as they rode up the steep track toward the bush, Zoe breathed in the fresh air, her skin tingling.

Below, the valley was a patchwork of fields, crops, and grasses, interspersed with steel sheds, their roofs glinting in the sunlight, while colourful, moving dots wandered spasmodically as they grazed.

Reaching the far corner of the farm, Claire leaned

over and opened the gate before whistling the dogs. 'Can you ride over there, Zoe?' Claire pointed to a level patch of grass twenty metres from the gateway. 'The dogs will bring the sheep to us, then I'll ride alongside them to stop them from spreading across the paddock. We want them to walk down to the yards by the wool-shed, keeping that fence on their other side. You can follow them up with Drum—he's good at keeping the rear of the flock together and won't let any escape. I'll take Harp, Bow, and Flute with me—and we'll keep our fingers crossed Bow behaves himself.'

Zoe grinned. As litter mates of Piccolo, both Bow and Echo were still pups and, although they had received weeks of instruction and experience with both Ginny and Claire, their puppy enthusiasm tended to override their listening skills—just as Piccolo's did.

But by the time Bow had galloped to the top of the paddock at Flute's side, his pace slowed and, panting, he seemed happy to trot at either Flute or Harp's heels, glancing regularly at Claire as she praised him.

Reaching for a handful of Tango's mane, Zoe leaned back in the saddle, her body swaying from side to side in rhythm with the horses as they descended the steep slope.

Walking at a quiet, steady pace, they reached the yards where the double gates were opened wide beside a gnarled pepperina tree.

Claire held her hand up in a stop signal for Zoe.

'Whoa, Tango.' She pulled the reins toward her belly, smoothly but firmly as Claire had taught her. The pony braked obligingly, her ears pricking forward as the flock of cream, woolly backs streamed through the opening and into the pen.

'Gidday!' Kirk called from the far corner of the yards. Approaching with his long-legged gait and stepping over each wood-and-steel set of railings as he reached them, he opened a gate from the large holding pen into a funnel-shaped smaller one that led into a long race.

While she and Claire dismounted, unsaddled their horses, and turned them loose in an enclosure shaded by a row of conifers, Kirk and Drum herded a portion of the flock into the race, packing the newly weaned lambs until they were comfortable but unable to turn around or lie down.

Zoe puzzled over this method briefly until Kirk began. With a backpack full of the sheep medicine on his back, a tube running from the canister to the pistol-like handpiece, Kirk began at the front of the flock and progressively worked his way backwards to the rear. The process appeared to Zoe to be slide hand under the animal's chin and lift head, squirt the measured quantity into the side of the lamb's mouth, release, shuffle backwards, and repeat. Astounded at the speed and efficiency of the process, she didn't hear Claire approach until she spoke.

'It's not always as easy as it looks.'

Zoe raised her eyebrows.

'Sometimes you get stubborn ones who drop their heads and hide by squishing under another's belly. When we do the rams and breeding ewes, it can be quite heavy work—especially with the knowing ones who do everything they can to get out of swallowing their medicine.'

Zoe chuckled then grimaced, picturing someone of her own small stature being overrun by the bigger sheep.

'Come on. He's nearly finished that lot. Would you mind nipping up the front and, as soon as Kirk gives you a wave, opening the gate on the left so the lambs can run out into the pen next door?' She indicated the three-way drafting system at the top of the race.

'Sure.' After striding across the mixture of soil, well-trodden sheep manure, and fallen leaves, she cautiously climbed over the top rail and positioned herself on the outside of the left-hand steel gate. Then, with a glance over the top of the flock to where Claire stood, she returned Claire's thumbs-up signal and waited.

Her mind drifted to the day she'd arrived in Featherwood Falls—the day she went for a walk feeling lost, angry, and afraid. Chuckling at her fear of the sheep in Emma's paddock that she had since learned were harmless, docile, and incredibly old, and absorbed in her recollections, she must have missed Kirk's wave, startling when Claire shouted, 'Zoe! Open the gate!'

Having hastily unclipped the latch and dropped the chain, she pulled the gate toward her, clinging to it as the lambs rushed past, leaping and bucking with their comrades at the potential freedom ahead.

The following hour flew past as the process was repeated until all lambs were dosed and stood in the shade of the woolshed.

'We'll leave them here while we have morning tea then take them to a fresh paddock,' Claire announced.

Kirk stripped the pack from his back and bent over the stainless-steel sink fixed to the side of the shed, scrubbing his hands and arms with a grey, rough-looking cake of soap.

Zoe pulled a face. His jeans were covered in lanolin stains, and frothy spittle peppered his shirt. Her legs and lower back ached from riding and—amazingly, she hadn't had a more interesting and rewarding morning in ages.

38

*E*mma welcomed Ryan with a weary hug. 'What a week,' she said, leaning into his solid, familiar body.

Despite the trauma of Lola's health scare and Zoe's disappearance, they had spent every waking moment together—and all of their sleeping hours. While Ryan supported his parents, working in the shop, post office, and on their smallholding, Emma weeded and watered her blossoming garden, and took Piccolo for long walks, sometimes with Zoe and other times with Ashleigh and Jazz. Her teaching friend had shared news and plans for hers and Damian's soon-to-be-built home in a cleared patch of bush on Dotty's property. Emma felt genuine happiness for both Ashleigh and Damian, without a skerrick of envy. While they walked, Ashleigh had prised tiny snippets of Emma's life from her—and Emma had surprised herself by being willing to share them.

Ryan interrupted her reflections, bringing her back to the present. 'Sure has been one out of the ordinary.'

'So, what's happening down at the shop? Is Lola resting like she's been told to?' She chuckled at Ryan's tilted head. 'Obviously not.'

'Actually, she's been better than I thought she'd be. It's given her a lift to have Zoe around, and the two of them seem to have formed a pretty tight relationship. Zoe's got her doing a massive jigsaw puzzle on the dining table and they've been watching reruns of *Friends* on TV. Mum's good in the morning but fizzles out around lunchtime, so that works well for Janet. She said she'd be happy to take on five afternoons a week plus all day Sunday if Mum will let her.'

Emma raised her eyebrows. 'And?'

'Mum's thinking about it.'

They shared a laugh while Emma made a pot of tea. Then they drifted onto the veranda, sitting companionably together on the tiny sofa and sipping at their drinks.

'Tomorrow,' he said, resting a hand lightly on her knee.

'Yes, tomorrow.'

'How do you feel about telling Zoe?'

'I don't think it will come as a surprise to her.' She

chewed at the corner of a fingernail as threads of nervousness attempted to worm their way inside her. 'It's early days, but she's got a wise head on her shoulders.'

'Unless a stranger comes visiting the shop, and she does a runner.'

Emma groaned and leaned her head on his shoulder. 'I know. Can you believe it? Tomorrow is New Year's Eve.'

'And what a great year it's going to be.' He took her empty mug from her and placed it on the glass-topped table next to his. Then he pulled her against him, and they kissed, softly at first, then, as the years of long-awaited passion rose inside her once again, she put her arms around his neck while he picked her up as though she weighed nothing and carried her to the bedroom.

'OH MY GOD ... how cool is that!' Zoe shrieked.

Emma was a bundle of nerves—worried Zoe might think she was stealing her newly discovered father away from her. But the moment Ryan announced he was moving in with Emma, she hugged them both tightly, her eyes glistening. Sharing the widest smile Emma had ever witnessed from her, Zoe whispered in her ear, 'I reckon you're the best couple ever. When you guys get around to getting married, can I be your bridesmaid?'

'Of course. That could be down the track a way though.' Emma grinned conspiratorially.

'That's okay. I can wait.'

'So, you don't mind me leaving you with Nan and Pop if I'm living with Emma?' Ryan asked.

Emma rubbed her hands down the sides of her slacks, her voice hesitant. 'You can move into the spare room here if you'd like to, Zoe. We could update it in whatever way you would like.'

'Huh,' Zoe snorted. 'Not likely. After twenty-five years, I reckon you two need some time alone. Anyway, I wouldn't like to leave Nan and Pop on their own now. I think they like me living there.'

Emma released the breath she hadn't realised she was holding. *Thank you, Zoe.*

'I guess that means we're not moving back to Brisbane, Dad.' Zoe's statement was matter-of-fact, as though the thought of life in Featherwood Falls no longer fazed her.

Emma decided it was possibly because Zoe's life had been rather nomadic—at least within the city limits. Perhaps Zoe valued a close-knit family more than anything? Emma wasn't sure, but whatever was going on in Zoe's mind, her support and blessing was all Emma needed.

'No,' Ryan said quietly. 'When we discussed our

stay in this village a few weeks ago, I didn't realise that Emma and I had a hope in hell of getting back together. I hadn't decided to quit my job ... and, well, I wasn't sure of anything, really. But ...' His gaze roved from one to the other. '... I think there's been a pretty big shift in emotions over the past couple of weeks, wouldn't you agree?'

Zoe crossed her arms over her chest, a worried scowl switching her expression from joyful amazement to solemn concern in a heartbeat. 'What if the police don't find that guy from the shop and he comes back?'

A brief frown flickered over Ryan's face. Stepping forward, he rested his hands on her shoulders. 'You're safe, Zoe. James and Rhys are working on the issue and will let us know when they have any news.'

'Are you sure?' she insisted testily.

'As sure as I can be. Your Nan said she and Janet will look after the shop and you need only help when you want to. I'm going to be working there as well— and sorting out the sheds and doing the accounts.'

Zoe bit her lip and nodded. 'Okay. So can we look at the schools as soon as they open again?'

'Of course we will. We'll download what we can regarding curriculum and subject choices, and the minute the school offices are open, we'll do a drive around them and get as much information as possible. Until then, though, Ginny and Claire have said you can spend as much time as you like at the farm.'

'And we'll begin the piano lessons, Zoe,' Emma added with a grin.

'Cool.' Zoe's demeanour changed again in an instant. 'I'm going to nip home and tell Nan and Pop.' She hesitated. 'Is that okay? Or is it a secret?'

Emma chuckled. 'I don't think it will surprise them so, yes, it's fine for you to tell them.'

Zoe shot them both a grin, bent to give Piccolo a quick pat on the head, and disappeared out the door.

THE FOLLOWING MORNING, Emma cast her eye over the tray of nibbles she had prepared, and for the tenth time, she peered through the oven's glass door at the tiny vol-au-vents. 'Although I've never spent Christmas dinner with the Shepherd family, I'm looking forward to tonight.'

'So am I—especially now.' Ryan caught her fingers in his and turned them over to study the dainty, pale-pink diamond set into a plain gold band that now adorned the third finger of her left hand. 'I can't get over how pleased Zoe was—and she hasn't seen the ring yet.'

Emma released a contented sigh, fingering the ring delicately with her right hand. 'And I can't believe you bought this so long ago—or that you've kept it.'

He shrugged. 'Yeah, well, it never crossed my mind

that you and I wouldn't marry, and I wanted to leave you with a material promise as well as a verbal one before I went west.' His voice trailed off. 'Only, when I bought this, I never dreamt that I would have to wait twenty-five years for that to happen.'

Emma looked up, tears threatening. 'I'll never forgive my mother for what she did—but I'm trying hard to put that behind me. From now on, I want us to look forward and enjoy every minute we have.'

He nuzzled into her neck as they hugged. 'Hear, hear.'

39

*L*ola placed the lemon meringue pie in the fridge next to the chocolate Bavarian cake and wiped her hands on a towel with a sigh. Stubborn determination wasn't always her best friend, but today she was grateful for it. With the niggling pains and breathlessness erased, thanks to the tiny, pristine tube allowing blood to pump to and from her heart, she had returned to her age-old habit of rising at six o'clock, determined to produce the best array of desserts for their belated Christmas dinner she'd ever made.

'What else would you like me to do, Nan?' Zoe burst through the adjoining house-shop door, letting it slam behind her in exactly the same way her father did. 'The washing is folded and put away and I've vacuumed the house.' A satisfied beam stretched across her face, reminding Lola of Ginny's kelpies when they knew their job was done and they required a pat of appreciation.

'Thanks, Zoe. You're a darling.'

Janet opened the door at the other end of the shop, her entry signalled by the now familiar, 'I'm here!'

At the sound of her assistant's voice, a balm of relief assuaged the anxiety that had woven its way through Lola. Reluctant to acknowledge her depleted energy levels and having counted down the minutes before Janet's expected arrival, she glanced up at the clock. 'Perfect timing.'

After exchanging pleasantries and minimal instructions, Lola hung her apron on the door and turned her back on the shop, passing through the entrance to her peaceful sanctuary—her home—while Zoe trailed behind her grandmother.

'Sit down and put your feet up, Nan. I'll make us a cup of tea.'

Gratefully accepting Zoe's fussing, Lola did as she was told, her heart giving a happy skip as her grand-daughter filled the kettle.

Placing the cup of tea in front of her grandmother, Zoe shot her a wry grin. 'You're easier to look after than Mum was.'

Bitterness tainted Zoe's voice, and Lola frowned. Drawing a deep breath, she grasped Zoe's hand, drawing her into the chair beside her. 'I understand how upset you've been with your mum's ... illness. But sometimes life is tough, Zoe—as you know.'

Zoe huffed. 'It was an addiction, not an illness.'

Lola waited for a few seconds before continuing. 'I didn't know your mother, but I'm a mother myself—and now a grandmother.' She smiled. 'A very happy one.'

Zoe met her gaze, the hint of a grin touching her lips.

'I know it's difficult to understand,' Lola added, 'but when things go horribly wrong and we find ourselves in a deep hole that we can't seem to escape from, we turn to ways of coping. Sometimes it's alcohol, sometimes it's talking to a professional, or someone we trust —and sometimes it's drugs. The problem is, when we begin our journey down this path, we don't always realise how easily our escape mechanism, or whatever the crutch is we find ourselves using, becomes habitual. Habits can become addictions and addictions can turn into an illness—often one we can't fight alone.'

Lola felt rather than saw Zoe squirm in her chair. Uncertain if she was poised for flight, she shot her a stern look as a small silence fell.

'It sounds to me that your mum found herself in that position, and because she had no one ...'

'She had me!' Zoe interrupted explosively.

'Yes, she had you. But you're her daughter, and she was your protector. I'm certain she would not have wanted to pour her troubles on you—not intentionally, anyway. Perhaps she simply couldn't summon the strength to find an alternative, and if she was worn down with a heavy workload and wasn't sure who she could trust enough to help, the illness would have consumed her.'

'She was an adult. She should have seen a doctor or someone.' Zoe's voice faded, choked with anger and unshed tears.

'I know, sweetheart.' Lola stood and wrapped her arms around Zoe, feeling the girl's sorrow pressing against her own heart. 'You loved your mum, and she loved you. But her illness was too powerful and ... she succumbed to the clutches of drugs.'

Zoe clung to Lola for several long minutes, as though needing to draw strength from the older woman.

'Tell me about when you were younger—before all this happened. What sort of places did your mother take you to? Did you ever go on a holiday?' Lola spoke quietly, desperate to direct Zoe's thoughts to happier times.

She shook her head. 'We didn't have holidays like Amy and Natalia did. Amy's family were always heading off camping and Natalia's went overseas a lot. But I remember going to the beach a couple of times. We'd get a unit overlooking the sea and spend most of the day swimming and exploring rock pools and stuff.'

A small smile touched her mouth and her shoulders straightened. 'We went to the movies quite often, especially during the school holidays when a new Disney movie came out.'

Gradually, hesitatingly, Zoe recalled more of the happier times from her childhood, and Lola felt the burden of agony fall away from the young girl's shoulders.

Eventually, she moved to the kitchen while Zoe stared at the wall, consumed in thoughts but with a vague smile on her face.

Lola made a fresh pot of tea and two ham-and-salad sandwiches. 'Come and sit on the couch with me. I think it's time we had a rest and watched another episode of *Friends* while we eat. Then it'll be time to get ourselves ready for this Christmas-come-New-Year dinner. This year, we've got lots to celebrate.'

Zoe pushed her chair back and took the plates from Lola's hands before resting them on the coffee table.

They slumped into the couches softness, surrounded by cushions, and Zoe leaned her head against Lola. 'Thanks, Nan. You're the best.'

40

*L*ight flooded the veranda and front path of the homestead, glistening on the lime-green leaves of the pistachio tree and highlighting the massive rose garden filled with blooms of every colour.

After parking next to Frank and Lola's car, Ryan dashed around to open the door for Emma while she balanced the tray of hors d'oeuvres on her lap.

As Zoe bounded out to greet them, Emma smiled at her stepdaughter-to-be, a little surprised how beautiful she looked after having mostly seen her in either ripped jeans or skinny leggings and a T-shirt. Sparkling turquoise eyes and a feminine summer dress seemed to have transformed the troubled teenager she had come to know and love. Or was it something more?

A breath of warm air rustled the shrubs beside the stairs, its soothing caress welcoming, reassuring.

'Hi, guys. Come and see the table. I decorated it while Ginny and Claire cooked the dinner.' Zoe beamed at them before dropping her gaze to Emma's left hand. 'Wow!' she squealed. 'Yesterday you were moving in together—and now you're engaged!' Filled with incredulity, her voice rose, drawing the attention of Kirk and Rhys, who were leaning over the railing, a beer in hand.

Ryan grinned at her while a flush crept up Emma's neck, no doubt highlighted by her fuchsia earrings and rose-coloured top.

Ginny and Claire appeared then, closely followed by Frank and Lola.

Placing the tray of food on the long, perfectly deco-rated table, Emma smiled shyly as congratulations were shared and hugs and back-slaps given.

'This calls for celebration,' Rhys said, reaching for a bottle of wine from the ice-filled esky in the corner.

With glasses filled and an inspection of Emma's ring conducted, they followed toasts with nibbles before another car drove in, its headlights beaming over the garden and its rapid halt sending dust parti-cles drifting into the hedge.

'Andrew's here,' Ginny announced.

'Is Sarah with him? Or his father?' Lola asked with trepidation.

Ginny shook her head vehemently. 'No, apparently Sarah had an invitation elsewhere, and as for his father, I believe he's long gone. Sarah told me at Christmas their divorce had been finalised and, because their farm was in joint names, she's bought him out. I think she intends to hand it over to Andrew and move into town. That's what she's always wanted —but I'm not sure how Andrew feels about it.'

Zoe returned to the gate before climbing the steps seconds later beside a laughing and attentive young man.

Although Emma had seen Andrew around and was aware of his new role as manager of Glenrowan, she had heard only negative stories about his father and was still digesting this latest piece of news from Ginny as the easy, loose-gaited man kissed Ginny and Claire on the cheek before roving around the table, smiling, and greeting everyone affably.

Sensing the familial bond between Andrew, his aunt, and cousin, the frisson of anxiety that had woven its way through Emma at the sight of his and Zoe's apparent friendship eased. It seemed his presence bore no relation to that of his father—whose lack of popularity was widely talked about in Featherwood Falls.

The evening wore on as glasses clinked, food was consumed, and conversation, laced with laughter, continued to flow.

A lengthy discussion ensued between Rhys, Claire,

Zoe, and Andrew regarding education, and Emma noted Zoe's intense interest in what they had experienced. Emma's hand rested in Ryan's, silently comparing Zoe's first days in Featherwood Falls and marvelling at the changes that a bare few weeks had brought to the confident young woman.

They had finished eating and were sitting back in their chairs, sipping glasses of wine or fruit punch, when Rhys's phone interrupted the conversation with its vibrant, intense ring tone.

He pushed his chair back, snatching it out of his pocket and glancing at the screen. 'Excuse me, guys, I need to take this call.'

Drifting into the garden, his murmured conversation blended with the croak of frogs and the racket of cicadas in the hedge.

Andrew, Claire, and Zoe cleared the table, stacked the dishwasher, and washed up the remaining utensils before returning to the veranda as Rhys leapt up the steps two at a time, his face pale and stony. 'Hey, Andrew. Can I have a word?'

Shooting a puzzled look at Rhys, Andrew followed him into the garden and across the lawn where they halted, resting arms on the timber-topped fence that surrounded the house-yard.

While it seemed like an age to Emma, they returned ten minutes later, Rhys's face solemn and Andrew's chalky—his grey eyes wide with shock.

'A problem?' Claire asked Rhys, a worried frown creeping across her forehead.

'Not really. More like ... the solution to a problem,' Rhys said.

'Now you're talking in riddles.' Claire's chuckle faded as her husband turned to Andrew, his head tilted questioningly.

'Tell them,' Andrew said bitterly. 'Better it comes from you than through the bush telegraph—with a heap of exaggerations.' He gazed around the table as the conversations faded, and they all glued eyes on Rhys.

'Go on, Rhys. Spit it out—it must be important,' Kirk said.

'That was James Avery. He apologised for ringing me on New Year's Eve but wanted to update me on an important matter—one that involves us.'

Emma turned her gaze to Zoe, her heart suddenly quivering as though stabbed with a blunt knife. She instinctively knew that whatever Rhys was about to share had something to do with the man whose voice had upset Zoe so much, and she fought the urge to ask Rhys to keep it to himself.

It was too late.

'They've got someone in for questioning about ... well, quite a few issues. Zoe's fears—and her statement —triggered red flags with a couple of matters James and the Feds have been working on.'

Emma's lips thinned as her eyes swept the table, an image of an Agatha Christie movie scene flashing through her mind. Puzzled frowns fixed themselves on every face, while Lola's jaw clamped tight, as though she, too, knew what was coming.

Rhys stared at Zoe. 'Something you said, Zoe, linked a whole heap of things together. Last year, we did a drug bust next door on Glenrowan, then we had an issue with wildlife smugglers in the area. But it was what one of the bikies said when I pulled them up before that—something that you reminded me of.'

There was not a sound from anyone at the table as, with nods and wide eyes, they encouraged him to continue.

He walked around and rested a hand on Andrew's arm. 'I'm really sorry, mate. The name both Zoe and those bikies mentioned was Dougie or Ducky. It was a long shot, but we put two and two together and worked out it could be a pseudonym for Donald Duck—or, in this case, Donald someone-else.'

'Donald Shepherd, my father.' Andrew spat, his eyes dark and flinty with anger.'

All faces turned from Andrew to Rhys again.

'Is this true?' Ginny asked, her voice shaking with incredulity.

'I'm afraid so. He's been on the watch list for a while, and now with Zoe's incident they had enough evidence to arrest him. He's in the watch house in Brisbane and his case will be heard in court the day after tomorrow. His vehicle was intercepted in Brisbane, returning from this district. The team searched the car and located more than two kilograms of amphetamines. We've established he had links with an outlaw motorcycle gang and was on his way to deliver the drugs to them on the Gold Coast. We believe he was moving his operation from this area to the coast. It was just lucky that he called into the store that day for a cup of coffee and Zoe recognised him.'

Ginny jumped to her feet and wrapped Andrew in a tight hug as silence gripped the air.

Emma dragged her gaze to Zoe's, meeting the girl's wide, horrified stare as Zoe pressed palms against her cheeks and choked, 'What have I done?'

41

*I*t was well into the night, with all ten of them comfortably seated in the roomy lounge of Featherwood Falls homestead, before a sense of calm settled over the group.

Kirk had disappeared immediately after Rhys's announcement, returning with a tray filled with glasses, a jug of water, ice—and a large bottle of whisky.

'I reckon this is the perfect time for some old-fashioned medicine.' He'd poured small quantities of the rich, dark liquid into glasses and passed them around, following up with offers of ice and water to dilute the potency.

Zoe coughed, choking on the tiny, watered-down mouthful her father had agreed might be helpful for her, and had decided after two gulps that, although a burning sensation had filled her throat, she felt less anxious and could focus on the shared reassurances that both she and Andrew had received.

Ginny had followed Kirk inside, returning with the phone and handing it to Andrew. 'It's your mum. I've told her everything, but James has already spoken with her. Now she wants to talk to you.'

Following the lengthy call, Andrew returned to the room, a resigned, solemn look on his face, the shock and anger now diminished.

'I'm glad Lyndon is no longer with us,' Ginny said quietly. 'He was so loyal and proud of the Shepherd family's achievements. From historic landholders to highly respected citizens in the area, he believed his family set a perfect example for others to follow.' She grunted then took a deep breath and lowered herself into an armchair. 'Look where that got us.'

Andrew squatted in front of her, taking one of her hands in his work-roughened one. 'Aunty Ginny, we both know what Dad's like. I might be his son, but you know as well as I do that we've never been close. I loved Uncle Lyndon and always felt more a part of this family than I did roaming around with my father while he either treated me like a slave or a prize bull. Why do you think I loved boarding school so much, even when I lived closer than any other boarders?' A steely edge crept into his voice. 'If I wasn't so proud of what you and Uncle Lyndon—and Briony and Claire—have achieved, I might be tempted to change my name by deed poll!'

A chuckle rose in his throat then, and a visible wave of relief washed through the room.

'And one thing we can all be thankful for is that the frightening and illegal goings-on that have tainted our little town will now stop,' Lola added.

'I'll drink to that.' Kirk grinned, picked up the whisky bottle, and began a round of top-ups.

Ryan put his hand over Zoe's empty glass. 'No more for you, my dear. One is enough.'

Like a snake coiled ready to strike, Zoe opened her mouth to object then, meeting her father's steely gaze, she grinned and rose to her feet. 'I'll make a pot of tea for Nan and me—and anyone else who's not allowed whisky.' She pulled a face and crossed into the kitchen, familiar with the homestead routine and equipment.

She glanced over her shoulder as she sensed someone behind her.

'I'll give you a hand,' Andrew said. 'And I reckon I'll join you in a cuppa, too.'

A flush of pleasure washed over her as she filled the kettle while Andrew reached into the overhead cupboard, spooned leaf tea into a teapot, and lined the mugs up on the bench.

'Please don't feel bad about what's happened, Zoe.' He spoke matter-of-factly, his words warmed by his smile. 'You've done a lot of people a good turn, especially Mum and me, and, even if I'm going to have to wear the stigma of my father's behaviour for a while, if you hadn't been honest and told Rhys everything, how many other lives might he have damaged?'

Surprised at his admission—and the relatively quick adjustment he seemed to have made in the hour or two since the phone call, his words soothed her, smoothing out the remnants of guilt that still clung in her mind.

Her hands rested against the bench while they waited for the kettle to boil, and he reached out and lay gentle fingers on hers. 'We'll get through this together, Zoe. You and me.'

She studied his kind face and nodded as the kettle clicked off, her smile spreading to reach her eyes. 'Thanks. I need a friend.'

'So do I,' he finished softly. 'Your Nan is watching us—probably wondering when her cuppa is coming.' He elbowed her gently and poured boiling water into the teapot while she removed the milk from the fridge. 'Come on, my friend, we've got tea to deliver, another slice of your grandmother's awesome cake to eat, and a world to conquer.'

She grinned at him, her heart soaring as he wrapped her in an affectionate gaze.

42

Three days later, Zoe pulled Tango to a stop beside Splash and the girls sat quietly while the horses stamped and swished flies, their long tails creating a rhythmic, shushing noise. Penny shot Zoe a puzzled frown before returning her gaze to Claire. Mounted on Akela, Claire seemed to be in a trance, oblivious to Drum's soft whimper and quivering body.

Behind them, a massive granite boulder that had been split in half lined either side of the narrow track the dogs had just pushed a mob of cattle through. Ahead of them, a kilometre or more away, a network of cattle yards filled the corner of the paddock. While beyond, nestled on the level crest before the land sloped toward the creek, the Featherwood Falls homestead stood, it's stone walls proud and strong.

To their left, the hill dropped away steeply, meeting the upper reaches of the creek as it trickled down toward the village.

'That's where my dad died,' Claire said quietly, pointing to the water.

Zoe's jaw dropped and she met Penny's wide eyes.

'How?' Zoe asked.

'He had an accident.' Claire huffed out a loud sigh. 'It was almost three years ago now. Long story. The neighbour wanted to buy a chunk of our land off us, Dad refused to sell, and the neighbour got angry and threw a rock at Dad.' She clamped her lips together while Zoe and Penny waited in horrified silence. 'Said he didn't mean to hurt my father, but it was too late. Dad had taken his helmet off and the rock hit his head, knocked him down the hill, and killed him.'

A stab of pain-filled guilt consumed Zoe. Claire had suffered as great a loss as she had and yet, until now, no one had mentioned how her father had died, and Claire hadn't breathed a word of the loss she must have felt.

'I'm so, so sorry to hear that, Claire,' Zoe said.

'What happened to the neighbour?' Penny asked.

Claire drew a deep breath and blew it out before answering. 'He's serving time for manslaughter. That's why Glenrowan needs a manager.' She looked down at Drum. 'Poor little Drum was the only witness. It's taken a long time for him to get his feet wet since then.

The culprit admitted he lost his temper, threw the rock and then, realising Dad was dead, dragged him into the water. We think Drum believes the water was responsible.'

'How awful for you all,' Zoe said.

Claire's shoulders sagged. 'Yeah. It was horrible, especially as it took a year to find the truth and have the neighbour arrested. Poor Mum went through hell.' She picked up her reins and squared her shoulders. 'Anyway, enough of history—we've got cattle to drench.' Turning to face both younger girls squarely, she continued, 'I'm sorry both of you have been going through a tough time—Zoe with your mum's death, and Penny with your parents' separation. Don't ever think I'm not feeling your pain. I am.' She finished with a compassionate smile. 'And we can all be here for each other. Agreed?'

Both Zoe and Penny nodded simultaneously, shooting Claire soft smiles.

Although it was a solemn descent to the cattle yards while Zoe dwelt on Claire's admission, a strength wove its way through her—a power she had not experienced before. Penny had been more friendly today, more humble and empathetic. Perhaps this was the sign they had both been waiting for, the sign of morphing from selfish teenagers to adults. Claire was right. They all had problems but sharing them made it easier.

THE CATTLE CRASHED against the steel bars surrounding them, mooing and grunting with dissatisfaction while Kirk leaned over the railings, spraying a liquid down each shiny, black back as they passed through the race. To Zoe, it was exhilarating chaos. While Claire operated the gate at the head of the lane, Ginny and the girls waved hats and shouted, "Move up, move up", urging the huge beasts ahead of them. The noise and activity demanded everyone's full concentration.

'Gidday!' Rhys yelled.

Penny noticed him first and pulled Ginny's sleeve. As the last group of cattle ran into the race, Ginny bolted the gate and climbed over the railing to greet Rhys. 'What's up?'

'Can I talk to you all?'

'Yeah. Hang on.' She put two fingers in her mouth and whistled shrilly, drawing the attention of both Kirk and Claire immediately.

After following Ginny and Penny over the rails and out into the paddock, Zoe stood in front of Rhys, an anxious frown on her face.

'I've got news,' Rhys said. He grinned at Zoe. 'Don't worry, Zoe. It's not bad.'

She shuffled from one foot to the other, anxiety building inside her.

'It's about Donald Shepherd,' Rhys said.

Zoe stifled a grunt.

'Thought you'd like to know he appeared in court yesterday and has been remanded in custody. Bail has been refused. The judge deemed him a potential risk. It seems he's worried he might interfere with witnesses and evidence, or try to disappear into his murky world, given his history.'

'So, when does the case get heard?' Ginny asked.

'It's set for mention at the end of this month.' Rhys turned to Zoe and smiled. 'You've got nothing to worry about, Zoe. Enjoy your holidays and don't give the whole thing another thought.'

Zoe's lip quivered as the tension she hadn't realised she'd been holding drained from her body. It was over —almost, anyway. She turned to meet the encouraging, supportive smiles of her friends. Only two months ago, she had known life would never be the same. But she had not expected the twists and turns it had taken. Now, standing in a paddock filled with rapidly drying grass, surrounded by a mob of bellowing cattle, she would never go back to being that bundle of nerves, waiting for adversity. She had a real future ahead of her—a wonderful family of her own, the prospect of a good education, and a village full of delightful friends.

*Z*oe was about to get into her father's car when Andrew's ute skidded to a halt outside the shop. 'Wow. You look pretty spiffy in that uniform.' He pointed a finger toward the ground and swivelled it, indicating she do a twirl.

Obligingly, she dropped her bag on the ground, held her arms out, and slowly rotated, displaying both front and back of her tartan dress, a grin on her face.

'Perfect. Nice hat too.'

She reached up to touch the traditional cream boater with the green band around it. 'And the shoes. Aren't they fashionable?' she laughed, pointing a black-leather, laced-up toe toward him.

'I brought you something,' he said, holding out a package wrapped in brown paper and tied with a pink ribbon.

'Really?' She took it from him, her eyebrows raised.

'You can open it. It's just a little thing I thought you might like.'

Sliding off the ribbon, she opened the parcel to reveal an A5-sized journal covered with a farm scene that included a flock of sheep grazing in a lush, green paddock with two horses being ridden in the distance. She peered closely at the riders, her eyes widening in surprise. 'That's Claire and me!'

'Yeah. You're hard to take photos of at that distance, but I wanted it to be a surprise.'

'So, you made the paper from a photo you took?'

'Yep. With a bit of help from Claire. I thought you might like to keep a journal. You know, write about the stuff that you enjoy—or don't, make notes about crabby teachers or school bullies you feel like punching.'

They were both laughing when Ryan appeared. 'We'd better go, Zoe, or you'll be late on your first day.'

She shot Andrew a grin, threw her bag on the back seat and climbed into the car. He leaned through the open window, giving her ponytail a playful tug. 'Have a great day—and if you get Mr Rowbotham as your maths teacher, tell him I said hi.'

She gave him a wave, rolled the window up, and sat back in her seat with a smile of both happiness and anticipation on her face.

EMMA STARED at the two pink lines darkening in the tiny white window of the plastic wand.

Shock and disbelief spiralled through her, and she put a hand on the bathroom bench to steady herself.

The queasy stomach, waves of nausea when she spooned Piccolo's food into her dish, and the inability to keep her eyes open after eight-thirty at night suddenly made sense.

Good grief. I'm forty-two and pregnant.

As shock eased, delight filled every part of her body. Then reality set in.

What will Ryan think? Our life together has only just begun.

She paced the garden, throwing the ball to Piccolo as she waited for Ryan's return. The school year had begun with a vengeance—another three new families adding seven students to the roll, and the hot, still days making playground duty an exhausting, sweat-inducing trial. The students' exuberance, however, had reminded her of how much she enjoyed her job, and how much she loved children.

At last, Ryan's vehicle approached. She waved, smiling as Piccolo raced ahead of her, leaping with excitement at Ryan's arrival. He parked in the carport behind her little car and hauled himself out before greeting the dog with a rub behind the ears and throwing the ball to the far corner of the yard.

Emma reached him, and they hugged. 'How did Zoe enjoy her first day?'

'Apparently, it was "pretty cool". She's made friends with a couple of girls who live this side of Warwick, and she's already been invited to join the choir. Apparently Penny also changed her mind about going back to Brisbane and, although is the year ahead of Zoe, is now attending the same school.'

Emma's eyes widened as he rushed on.

'Before I forget, Mum wants us to come for dinner. Enough about the family. How was your day?'

Clasping his hand in hers, Emma dragged him toward the house. 'I've got something to show you.'

Mystified, he angled his head, raising an eyebrow as he followed her inside.

She filled the kettle, her back to him while he settled onto a bar stool. With the tea made, she sat next to him and fixed her eyes on the white pregnancy test resting only centimetres from his elbow, clearly unnoticed.

Before she took her first mouthful, he said, 'What is it you want to show me?'

Rolling her eyes, she shoved it in front of him.

For a few moments, he stared at it, his brow furrowed, then he lifted his gaze, his face alight with wonder. 'This isn't a covid test. Is this one a pregnancy test?'

'Yep. It's a bit of a shock, isn't it?'

He breathed slowly in and out, in and out, while her stomach did somersaults and she steeled herself for the disappointment.

His smile spread, erasing the lines that channelled his cheeks.

They both laughed while Piccolo stared at them with a questioning gaze.

'This is the best news I've ever had.'

As EMMA and Ryan arrived at the side of the shop, Rhys pulled up beside them in the police wagon. 'Gidday,' he said. 'You guys got a minute?'

'Sure. Come inside,' Ryan answered, pushing the gate open and waving Rhys through ahead of him and Emma.

A few minutes later, with the extended Brown family seated in the living area, Rhys cleared his throat. 'I've come straight from the farm and thought you'd like to hear the latest news, too.'

Lola sat forward, her gaze trained on Rhys. 'Is this about the court case? It was today, wasn't it?'

He nodded. 'Yes. Donald Shepherd indicated he will

be pleading guilty, so the case will not go to trial. Further news is that detectives have tracked down Adrian, who has admitted that he supplied methamphetamine to Catherine and that he has been supplying numerous others with the drug that was given to him by Donald. The case is now very tightly wrapped around Donald, and I believe this is why he has entered the plea of guilty.'

'Does that mean none of us will have to go to court?' Zoe asked.

'Yes, Zoe.'

'So, just how serious are Donald's charges—and what are they?' Frank asked.

'Unfortunately, they haven't been able to present evidence of any link to wildlife smuggling. The couple who are already serving time for that are staying quiet, but we still believe he had a hand in it. But there's plenty of proof he's one of the main ringleaders for the manufacturing and supply of drugs, if not the main "lord". James and his team are still producing witness statements, especially now so many events can be linked.'

He gave Zoe a soft smile. 'Don't worry, Zoe. You're quite safe. He won't be let out of jail any time soon and, hopefully, if the judicial system does its job, he will go down for a lengthy period.'

Lola sat back on the couch and released a long, noisy breath. 'How's Andrew taking all this?'

'Okay—under the circumstances. He's going to

continue taking care of Glenrowan. Says he wants to prove to the community that the Shepherd family are good and honest citizens and that he will not let one bad apple in the family taint them all.'

Lola nodded approvingly as Rhys got up to leave and glanced at the dining table where covered dishes were leaking delicious hints of their contents. 'Sorry to have kept you all from your dinner.'

Ryan stood, but Rhys held his hand up. 'I'll let myself out. Enjoy your meal—and a good night's sleep.' Then, closing the door behind him, he disappeared.

The room was silent except for the clatter of cutlery against china for several minutes as they served food and took their seats.

They had finished the main course, and Zoe got up to clear the plates when Ryan gestured to her to sit down. 'Emma and I have got some news,' he said.

'Oh. You've set the date for your wedding?' Zoe said, pressing the tips of her fingers together and raising her eyebrows in anticipation.

'Not yet,' Emma mumbled. 'It's something a bit more ... challenging.'

Zoe angled her head in question.

'We're having a baby,' Emma said.

Complete silence filled the room for several long seconds before both Lola and Zoe exploded with happiness at the same time.

They shared congratulations and hugs before Emma advised, 'I don't even have a due date yet—or confirmation that everything is okay.' But despite her warning, she couldn't stop smiling.

'I'm going to be a sister!' Zoe shrieked with the delight of a child before squeezing Emma for a second time. 'And I couldn't wish for a nicer stepmother.'

'It will be fine, Emma,' Lola said quietly, flapping a hand at Zoe as if that would calm her excitement. 'It's been an event-filled three months and we've all had our fair share of problems. This time though, I'm sure everything will be perfect—and we couldn't be happier.' I'm going to be a grandmother again!'

As Lola lay a hand on her chest silently as though she were giving a prayer of thanks, Piccolo, who had been patiently sitting on her mat in the corner of the room, lifted her head and let out a joyful yodel.

Outside, a brushtail possum growled—the rattly call almost drowned out by laughter.

Zoe leaned over her grandmother's shoulders, hugging her gently as she smiled across the table at her father. 'Thank you for saving me,' she whispered.

'You're welcome.'

ACKNOWLEDGMENTS

There is an old African saying: "It takes a village to raise a child".

While I live in Australia, those few words speak volumes. As the author of this book, I claim it to be mine, but I could not have got it to this stage without my helpful team of family and friends.

To my beloved husband and sisters, I value your encouragement, support and honest critique above all else and thank you from the bottom of my heart. Your suggestions, constructive comments and tolerance make the relatively lonely career of writing worthwhile.

To Anna and Lauren at CREATINGink, thank you both for editing my books. Your expert assistance and ongoing friendship is both respected and revered.

Patti Roberts at Paradox Book Cover Designs—thank you again for your gorgeous covers and so much more.

Readers, I hope you have enjoyed reuniting with Lola and the Featherwood Falls community in addition to getting to know both Emma and Zoe. Thank you for reading my books.

Featherwood Falls is looking forward to greeting you again!

ALSO BY HEATHER REYBURN

Tullagulla Series

The Cedar Tree

The English Oak

The Pepperina Grove

A Tullagulla Christmas

Fantail Ridge Series

Peninsula Promises

The Lupin Fields

The Scent of Promise

Featherwood Falls Series

A Stranger in Featherwood Falls

Secrets in Featherwood Falls

Sparks Fly in Featherwood Falls

Clouds over Featherwood Falls

A STRANGER IN FEATHERWOOD FALLS

To lose a loved one is tragic, but to lose a lifetime of dreams? Unthinkable.

Alone on a two thousand hectare sheep and cattle property, Ginny Shepherd questions her husband's sudden death, convinced it was no accident. As a series of farm related incidents unravel, heightening her suspicions, her livelihood is put under threat. Featherwood Station is Ginny's lifeblood—her passion, her home, and her haven and she is determined it will stay that way. But it seems someone else wants the property as much as she does and will stop at nothing to get it.

When a stranger finds a forgotten token gifted to him as a child, distant memories set him on a path to pursue his grandfather's dream. But, greeted with more questions than answers, he finds life in the heart of

Queensland's Granite Belt more difficult than expected.

A smouldering attraction forms between he and Ginny, alarm bells sound and frightening events escalate. Ginny's life is in danger.

Is the stranger who he says he is? Or could it be that someone has a grudge to settle?

SECRETS IN FEATHERWOOD FALLS

A small country town. A conscientious cop. And a whole lot of secrets.

Constable Rhys Morton is new to Featherwood Falls and knows one thing for certain—he wants to remain in this village as much as he wants to remain a cop. But just as he uncovers troubling historical information, an accusation threatens his security and he must weigh up his options. Should he pursue the cold case and risk ruffling powerful feathers, or protect his future and a budding romance?

Claire Shepherd is still reeling from her father's death and when fresh heartbreak strikes, she seeks peace in the haven of Featherwood Station, her childhood home. Sparks fly between Claire and the new cop in town and she is torn between her dream of managing her father's legacy or falling for a man whose position is only temporary.

Alarm bells chime when new neighbours move in. Is this little town the sleepy hollow Rhys believed it to be? Desperate to uncover local secrets, he seeks Claire's help. After all, she knows the area and he has nothing to lose—except his heart.

Secrets is Rhys and Claire's story and the second in the Featherwood Falls series.

SPARKS FLY IN FEATHERWOOD FALLS

Fed up with life under scrutiny, Ashleigh Paton considers her grandmother's favourite saying—
"Escape to the Country! A Change is as good as a holiday."

The advice ignites a yearning in Ashleigh to leave city life and all it involves. A teaching position in Featherwood Falls could provide the answer, one she hopes will offer the new life she craves. After all—what could go wrong? It's better than being unemployed and the reward could be the peace she desires.

Damian Cartwright has a secret. Like his eccentric great-aunt, a reclusive life in the bush suits him. Except now his son, Charlie, is old enough to start school, and old enough to be subjected to ridicule. It's time for action, even if that involves calling a truce with Charlie's feisty new teacher.

When unexplained events occur in the area, young

Charlie forces Ashleigh into seeking answers. But uncovering the truth proves more shocking than imagined and sparks fly in more ways than one.

Can Ashleigh extinguish the inferno without destroying all she has gained? Or will her dreams be over before they begin?

Sparks Fly in Featherwood Falls is the third book in this series.

ABOUT THE AUTHOR

Heather Reyburn enjoyed an idyllic childhood in beautiful New Zealand, before settling on the Darling Downs in Queensland. With a passion for nature, animals, reading and all things farm related, it wasn't long before her rural lifestyle inspired dreams of writing stories of her own. She loves happy endings, history, suspense, and characters who remain with the reader long after "The End". When not writing, Heather is often found in the garden or spending time with her husband and family.

  BB